Int.

by

Jay Northcote

To Lindsay
Thanks for being
an awesome
reader :)

Love
Jay N
x

Copyright

Cover artist: Garrett Leigh.
Editor: Sue Adams.
Into You © 2016 Jay Northcote.

ALL RIGHTS RESERVED

This literary work may not be reproduced or transmitted in any form or by any means, including electronic or photographic reproduction, in whole or in part, without express written permission.
This is a work of fiction and any resemblance to persons, living or dead, or business establishments, events or locales is coincidental.
The Licensed Art Material is being used for illustrative purposes only.
All Rights Are Reserved. No part of this may be used or reproduced in any manner whatsoever without written permission, except in the case of brief quotations embodied in critical articles and reviews.

Warning
This book contains material that is intended for a mature, adult audience. It contains graphic language, explicit sexual content, and adult situations.

Acknowledgements

As always this story was brought to you with the help of lots of wonderful people. Thank you to my editor Sue Adams, for making my words better; my alpha/beta readers and writing companions Annabelle Jacobs, R.J. Scott and Lennan Adams for keeping me going and not letting me give up; and my proof readers: Stacy, Con Riley, N.R. Walker and Jen for the final polishing. And last but not least, thank you to my supportive and long-suffering family for helping me talk through plot points and timeline issues, and for putting up with me being grouchy and demanding when my deadline was approaching. I love you.

PROLOGUE

August 2009

"Oh, Scott!" Olly threw his hands up in frustration as the football sailed over his head, a dark silhouette against the blue summer sky before it disappeared over the fence behind him.

"Oops." Scott grimaced.

This was the second time they'd lost the ball today. The first time had been Olly's fault—an overzealous kick sending the ball into the garden on the other side. The Parkers, who lived there, were both out at work, so Olly had climbed over the fence to rescue it.

"You have to go and knock on Miss Wychwood's door." Olly looked nervously over his shoulder at the fence. "We can't just go and get it, because she'll be in."

Scott's brow furrowed. "Will you come with me?"

"No way. She gives me the creeps. You were the one who kicked it over."

Olly's mum always told him there was no reason to be scared of Miss Wychwood.

She's just a harmless old lady. She's probably lonely, Olly.

But Olly didn't like the way Miss Wychwood stared at him when he passed her in the street. It was like she could see all his secrets, including the deepest, darkest ones he didn't share with anyone—not even Scott.

Scott rolled his eyes. "Well, I'll climb over and get it, then. I'll be in and out before she notices."

"No!"

2

It was too late; Scott had already grabbed the top of the fence and jumped, hauling himself up. "I won't be a minute."

Olly wiped the sweat from his brow. It was a hot August day, one of many in the long summer holidays, and they'd been out in the sun for ages. After a few minutes there was still no ball and no sign of Scott returning.

"Did you find it?" Olly called.

"Not yet" came the reply. "It's like a jungle over here. Come and help?"

Olly heaved a huge sigh. Typical Scott. He always rushed into things and then dragged Olly along with him because Olly couldn't say no to him.

Despite his misgivings, Olly scaled the fence and dropped down the other side into the tall shrubs that flanked the edge of Miss Wychwood's garden. Suddenly cool in the shade of the plants rising above his head, Olly blinked as his eyes adjusted to the dimmer light. It *was* like a jungle. Flowering shrubs and vines grew close together forming archways of green that blocked the sun. The sweet, heady scent of the blooms wrapped around Olly's senses and the hum of bees and other insects made him feel as though his brain was buzzing.

He peered through the undergrowth. "Scott?" he hissed.

"Over here. Look, I found a frog."

Olly pushed through the gap in the bushes to find Scott squatting beside a small pond where bright orange fish lurked in the green water and a frog sat on a lily pad.

3

"Yeah. Awesome. But you're supposed to be looking for the football." The skin prickled on the back of Olly's neck. This garden was an amazing place, and if they'd had permission, he'd have liked to explore it more. But they didn't. They shouldn't be there, and he wanted to get back to his side of the fence before they got in trouble. "Look, we're never going to find it. Let's get back over my side, and I'll go and knock on her door—which is what you should have done in the first place."

"Is this what you're looking for?"

The quavery voice made Olly's heart leap into his throat. Even Scott jumped up, his eyes wide.

Olly wheeled around to see Miss Wychwood with Scott's football clasped in her bony, wrinkled hands. In the soft green light of the undergrowth, she was almost part of her garden. Her fingers were like twigs, and her wild, tangled hair mirrored the vines that twisted overhead. As she stared at them, her eyes were green and piercing, but her expression was mild.

Scott found his voice first. "Oh, I'm sorry. We, um…."

As the shock subsided, Olly was able to help him. "We didn't want to disturb you, so we thought it would be easier if we climbed over to get it. I'm really sorry, Miss Wychwood." His face flamed. He knew it was a weak excuse. His mum and dad would be furious with him if she told them about this.

"How thoughtful of you, dear." There was a glint in her eye that might have been amusement.

4

Olly was aware of Scott standing beside him. All his boldness seemed to have evaporated. It was stupid, really. Miss Wychwood was tiny and frail. Scott, tall for his eleven years, must be a good couple of inches taller than she was. How did she manage to be so alarming?

Olly reached to take the ball from her hands. There was a moment of resistance before she released it, as though she wasn't going to let go.

He tucked it under his arm and ran his free hand through his sweaty mop of dark hair. "So... we're sorry we bothered you. We'd better go."

He made no move to leave, unsure whether they should climb back over the fence. It seemed rude to do that now, but the only alternative was to go through her house.

"You look hot, Olly. Scott too."

Olly wondered how she knew Scott's name. Perhaps she'd heard them yelling at each other as they played. Best friends since preschool, they'd grown up in and out of each other's homes and gardens.

"Come and have some lemonade. I just made a batch, and some shortbread too."

She turned and began to make her way through the overgrown plants towards the house, stooping and shuffling a little as she walked.

Olly glanced sideways at Scott, who shrugged.

Either they legged it back over the fence and risked annoying her even more by being rude, or they followed. Olly's parents had always been very hot on stranger danger, never accepting lifts, and stuff like that. But Miss Wychwood had lived next door since before he was born, his parents were on good terms with her, and he didn't think the warnings applied to tiny old ladies anyway.

"Come along," she called back briskly.

The sunlight was dazzling as they crossed a small patio on the back of the house. As they followed her indoors, cool darkness enclosed them again.

It was almost like stepping back into the garden. The walls were a dark muted green and there were houseplants everywhere, drooping in tangled trails from the mantelpiece and lined up on the windowsill. The sweet smell of baking made Olly's mouth water.

"Have a seat." She gestured to an ancient-looking sofa. "I'll be back in a moment."

The sofa sagged as they sat on it, pushing them together in the middle. Olly didn't mind being squashed up next to Scott; the warmth of his body was comforting.

"I don't like this," Scott whispered.

"Me neither. But I'm sure she's harmless."

Scott didn't look convinced. "What's that?" He pointed to a large sphere resting on a wooden stand on the mantelpiece. I looked as if it was made of glass, or maybe crystal, but it was opaque, the insides filled with strands of misty grey. "It's like a—"

Just then an imperious *miaow* demanded their attention, and a large, black cat jumped onto the sofa next to Olly and rubbed its head against his arm, demanding to be stroked. Olly recognised the cat, which sometimes sat on the wall at the front of the house. He often paused to say hello to it on his way to and from school. The cat seemed to remember him.

"Oh, Rowan. He's such a softie." Miss Wychwood was back with a heavily laden tray containing a large jug of yellow liquid, three glasses, and a plate of shortbread biscuits.

6

She smiled fondly at the cat, and suddenly she seemed softer and less intimidating. Olly relaxed a little.

Once she'd given them glasses of sweet-sharp homemade lemonade and plied them with delicious, crumbly shortbread, Olly had completely changed his opinion of Miss Wychwood. Even Scott had opened up and was answering her questions. Rowan had stepped over Olly and curled up on Scott's lap, purring contentedly as Scott tickled him under the chin.

Scott explained they'd finished primary school now and would be moving on to Fairfield, the local secondary school, in September. "We're going to be in the same tutor group." Scott glanced sidelong at Olly and smiled.

Olly grinned back. They'd both been over the moon when they found that out.

"So, you two are best friends, then?" She looked from one to the other, her eyes bright in her wrinkled face. "Best friends are a special thing. A friendship that lasts is truly precious, but sometimes it's hard to hold on to friendships as you grow and change. I hope you boys grow together rather than apart."

Her words made something ache behind Olly's breastbone. He'd always taken Scott's presence in his life for granted. The suggestion that he might not have Scott as a friend forever was alien and unwelcome. He opened his mouth to argue, to assure her there was no way they'd grow apart.

Scott beat him to it. "Of course we'll always be friends. We made a promise. We're going to be best friends forever." He was frowning, his cheeks flushed.

Olly fingered the tiny scar on his wrist and remembered the day they made their pact. They were nine years old, and Scott had just got a penknife for his birthday. Olly had been incredibly envious of it because his mum wouldn't let him have one.

"Well, that's good, then," Miss Wychwood said mildly. "You see you both keep your promise. A blood vow is powerful magic. It can never be broken."

How did she know? Olly thought.

There was no way she could know what they'd done. Nobody knew about it apart from him and Scott. Their parents would have gone mental if they'd found out they'd cut themselves on purpose.

"Magic isn't real," Scott said. But the words came out sounding uncertain, as though there was a question mark at the end of them.

Sitting here, surrounded by growing things in this strange room, with Miss Wychwood's penetrating gaze on them, Olly wasn't sure what to believe anymore. Unease swept through him again. This had been a bad idea. They should never have climbed over her fence. His gaze lit on the strange glass ball on the mantelpiece again. Maybe it was a trick of the light, but it looked as though the mist inside it was moving, re-forming into constantly changing shapes.

He cleared his throat and stood. "I think we should go. My mum'll be home soon. She only popped out to the supermarket, and she'll worry if we're not there when she gets back."

"Yeah." Scott lifted Rowan carefully off his lap and stood too. "Thank you for the lemonade and biscuits."

At least one of them remembered their manners. Olly was too jittery to think straight. He nearly forgot to pick up the football that had landed them there in the first place.

Miss Wychwood made no objections and showed them to the front door. She paused in the gloomy hallway. "It was lovely to meet you both properly at last after all these years of seeing you coming and going in the street. Two best friends." She smiled. "Maybe one day you'll be even more than that."

Olly frowned, not sure what on earth she was talking about. "Okay. Well, thank you. And I'm sorry we climbed over your fence without asking."

"Oh, that's quite all right." She opened the door and bright light flooded in, chasing away the shadows.

They stepped out into the August heat, and Olly breathed a sigh of relief as the door closed behind them. Out in the sunshine with the blue sky above them, normality was restored and he felt silly for being so unsettled by a harmless old lady. The whole incident already seemed unreal, like a dream.

"Hey." Scott nudged him. "You wanna go and play more football?" His grin was wide and his eyes matched the summer sky.

Olly smiled back. "Yeah. Only, let's try and keep the ball in my garden from now on."

CHAPTER ONE

Seven years later. April 2016

On his way home after the first day back at school after Easter, Olly was cycling along and enjoying the late-spring sunshine. He'd just turned into his road and was nearly at his house.

The roar of the engine was all the warning he got before a shiny red Ford shot past him, far too fast and far too close. He instinctively lurched away from it, hit the kerb, and went flying off his bicycle.

"Ow." He examined the rip on his jeans and a large scrape on his knee beneath the hole. His pride was hurt more than his leg, and as the car screeched to a halt and Scott got out, the adrenaline from the fall surged in Olly's system and turned into white-hot rage.

Staggering to his feet, he drew himself up to his full height—which was, annoyingly, several inches shorter than Scott, the fucking freak of nature—and yelled. "You idiot! You took the corner way too fast. You could have killed me."

"Yeah. I'm sorry." Scott held his hands up. He had the grace to look guilty, at least, but that didn't make Olly feel any better. "Are you okay?"

Scott's latest girlfriend, Amy, had got out of the car now too and was gawping at them. The sight of her stoked Olly's anger higher.

10

"No, I'm not okay. I'm bleeding. And these jeans are—*were*—my favourites." Four years of resentment poured out of him. "How the hell did you manage to pass your driving test? You've clearly got no fucking road sense." It stung that Scott had passed his test first time when Olly had failed twice. Even when Olly did eventually pass, he would only have access to his mum's old banger. Scott's parents had bought him his own car for his eighteenth birthday. It was so unfair.

Scott bristled. "Fuck you. I'm a perfectly good driver. I just didn't see you. It could have happened to anyone."

"Anyone who's blind and stupid, sure," Olly snapped.

They glared at each other, fists clenched and breathing hard. Scott's jaw was set in a tense line, and Olly hated how attractive he found him. Anger, desire, and hurt coiled in his stomach, a nauseating and shameful cocktail. If he knew how to throw a decent punch, he'd do it. Right into Scott's stupid, beautiful face. But knowing Olly's luck, he'd probably break his hand.

"Boys, boys, boys."

In the tension of the moment, neither of them had noticed Miss Wychwood approaching. She stood, leaning on her stick as she studied them. Her black cat was there too, sitting by her ankles, with his yellow-eyed gaze fixed on Olly.

"What happened to those two young men who were going to be best friends forever?" She shook her head sadly.

If Olly didn't know better, he'd swear the cat looked equally disappointed in them. "They grew up," he replied with acid in his tone.

It was painful being reminded of their friendship, and it was none of her bloody business anyway. He glared at Scott again, and Scott stared back. The anger had gone from his blue eyes, replaced by something that looked like regret. That only made Olly more irritated. It was too late for regret. There was no going back to what they'd been.

"But this isn't what fate had in store for you." Miss Wychwood's words drew Olly's attention back to her. She was frowning as though trying to solve a particularly difficult puzzle. "This isn't how it's supposed to be."

"What's she talking about?" Amy asked.

Miss Wychwood ignored her, still staring at Olly and Scott, and shaking her head.

Olly didn't have time to humour a crazy person. Blood was trickling down his leg, his hip ached where he'd bruised it as he landed, and he wanted to get away from all of them—including the damn cat, which was still staring at him. "Whatever. I'm going now."

With as much dignity as he could muster, he picked up his bike from where it lay twisted in the road. Thankfully it didn't seem badly damaged. He straightened the handlebars.

Miss Wychwood's cat had moved away from her ankles and was sitting, blocking his path.

"Shoo," Olly said, wheeling the bike closer to the creature until his front wheel was almost touching it.

The cat blinked, its yellow eyes like headlamps, and then it flicked its tail and sauntered away so he could pass.

Olly tried not to limp as he pushed his bike down the road to his driveway. He dumped it outside his house and then let himself in without looking back.

12

Fucking Scott and his stupid girlfriends.
Bloody nosey old woman.
Pain-in-the-arse cat.

The day officially sucked sweaty donkey balls. As Mondays went, it was one of the worst he could remember in a while.

Scott watched Olly's retreating form. Even though he'd said he was okay, he was obviously sore. Guilt poked insistently at Scott's belly because Olly was right—Scott *had* been going too fast. Carried away by the thrill of driving his own car, he'd been careless. It was lucky for both of them it hadn't been more serious. The thought of what could have happened to Olly made Scott feel nauseous, not to mention his dad would probably kill him if he damaged the car when he'd had it less than a month.

He sighed. Olly was going to hate him more than ever now, and he was tired of Olly's antagonism and scorn. He rubbed at his wrist, fingers instinctively finding the tiny notch of the scar he'd made the day they swore to be friends forever.

So much for promises.

Scott never understood why Olly had cut him off so brutally. Even four years later, it still hurt that Olly had cast him aside as if their friendship meant nothing. Scott wasn't stupid; he knew it was something to do with the kiss. It had been a weird night that had left Scott feeling confused, but he still didn't get why Olly dumped him as a friend right after it.

"This isn't how it's supposed to be," Miss Wychwood said again, drawing Scott's attention back.

There was a troubled expression on her face.

"Sorry, what?" Scott frowned. What was the mad old bat on about?

She carried on as though Scott hadn't spoken, talking to herself more than to him, with a faraway look in her eyes. "The crystal never lies." She shook her head. "But sometimes fate needs a helping hand."

With that, she turned and walked away with the black cat at her heels.

Scott's skin tingled with a chill of unease. He shook it off, telling himself not to be daft. She was clearly a few sandwiches short of a picnic.

"Come on, Scott." Amy tugged at his arm, reminding him of her presence. "Let's go."

They got back into his car. Scott started the engine and drove—very carefully—to park outside his house at the end of the road.

Once they were inside the house, Amy started interrogating him, following him as he walked into the kitchen. "Who was that old lady?"

"She's just a neighbour. She lives next door to Olly."

"Does she have, like, dementia or something?" Amy wrinkled her nose. "She was really odd. She gave me the creeps."

"I don't know. I think she's always been a bit strange." Scott remembered the time they'd climbed over her wall. Miss Wychwood had said some weird stuff that day too.

"And why has Olly got such a problem with you? Didn't you two used to be friends?"

"That was years ago," Scott said shortly, pouring some orange juice for himself. "Do you want a drink?"

"Have you got any Diet Coke?"

"No, sorry."

14

"Just water, then, please."

They took the drinks up to Scott's room. Amy kicked her shoes off and lay on his bed. She patted the space beside her. "Come on."

Scott looked at his clock. "My parents will be home soon."

"But they're not here now, and we'll hear the front door."

Unsettled, Scott wasn't in the mood for fooling around. But he'd only been seeing Amy for a couple of weeks and they hadn't got much beyond the snogging stage, anyway. Last week he'd groped her boobs a bit, and she'd rubbed him through his trousers. Then his mum had come home and they'd had to stop. His parents insisted on him keeping the door to his room open if he had a girl in there. Scott had been relieved rather than disappointed at the interruption, but he tried not to think too much about why.

He lay down beside Amy and kissed her, because he knew it was what she wanted. She responded enthusiastically. Her lips tasted of fruity lip balm, and her long nails scratched his scalp as she slid them into his hair. She made a little breathy moan. It should have been hot, yet just like always, Scott was left feeling as if something was missing.

Amy was the latest in a long line of girlfriends. None of them ever held his interest, and deep down, Scott knew why, even though he didn't like to admit it to himself.

His mind drifted back to his argument with Olly, the anger and resentment on Olly's face, and Miss Wychwood's words.

This isn't how it's supposed to be.

15

Once Scott's mum got home—interrupting them again before any clothes came off—Amy left. She only lived a few streets away, so Scott walked her home and kissed her goodbye on her doorstep.

"I wish your mum worked later." She sighed. "It's so annoying that we hardly ever get to be alone together."

"Yeah." Scott tried to look suitably disappointed. He'd secretly been quite glad when his mum had put a stop to their groping again. He hadn't got hard while they were kissing, and if they'd gone far enough for Amy to notice, she'd probably have been offended.

When he got back to his house, he was feeling restless and antsy. His mum was in the kitchen, chopping vegetables.

"Have I got time for a run before dinner?"

"Yes. We won't be eating for about an hour."

"Okay, thanks."

Scott changed into running clothes, put on his iPod, and turned up the volume loud. As he ran down the street, he passed Olly's house. He couldn't help glancing at the front window, but he couldn't see inside. He hoped Olly was okay.

Miss Wychwood was in her front garden, stooping over a flowering shrub with a pair of secateurs. She glanced up as Scott ran past and she nodded in greeting, a thoughtful look in her eyes. He gave her a half-hearted smile and picked up his pace.

16

He ran fast, pushing himself to his limits. His body was strong, fit from regular football training, and he loved the burn in his muscles and the pounding of his heart. It made all the tensions of the day drop away into nothing. All that mattered was the physical sensation; there was no space left to worry or to think too hard about anything.

He did a long loop around the small town where he lived, circling the park and taking the cycle path that ringed the new builds at the edge of town. Forty-five minutes and a few miles later, he turned back into his cul-de-sac and started to sprint the last couple of hundred yards to his front door.

"Fuck!" He almost tripped over Miss Wychwood's cat as it shot out of her garden, like a black shadow, and crossed the pavement just inches from his feet.

Bloody cat!

The surge of adrenaline only helped him run faster, and by the time he got back to his own front door, his lungs were on fire. He leaned against the wall to stretch out his calf muscles; the sweat poured down his face. Exhilarated and exhausted, everything felt better than it had before his run.

After showering, Scott laid the table while his mum finished cooking.

"Where's Dad?"

"Running late. His train was delayed, but he called me from the station. He should be here any minute."

Sure enough, Scott's dad arrived as his mum was dishing up. He came straight into the kitchen, dressed in his suit, rumpled from his daily commute to and from London. "Sorry, darling." He kissed Scott's mum on the cheek.

"How was your day?" she asked.

"Long and tiring. Yours?"

"Same."

Once they were sitting at the table with their food in front of them, Scott's dad started grilling him about schoolwork—as usual.

"How was your first day back at school? I hope you're ready to work hard this term."

Scott replied politely. "It was fine, thanks."

"Are you keeping to the revision timetable you made? What did you do after school today? Or was it a football training day?"

Scott finished his mouthful before he answered. "No, that's tomorrow. I saw Amy for a while. Then I went for a run." Scott saw his dad's jaw tighten, so he added quickly, "But I'm going to do two hours of Biology tonight—straight after dinner. I've got a past paper to work through."

"Good." His dad nodded. "The sooner the football season ends the better. It worries me that you're still spending so much time with sports. The next couple of months are so important."

Scott gritted his teeth. He didn't need his dad to tell him. Nobody wanted him to get the grades he needed to go university more than he did. Good A level results were his ticket out from under this roof and away from his domineering father. "We've only got two more weeks of football anyway. It's the school county final on the last weekend of April, and then we're done."

"About time. I think it's ridiculous they let you play in your final year at all. You should be focused on studying, not running around a football pitch. Jamie gave up sports in the sixth form, and it paid off."

Scott didn't answer, and thankfully his father stopped going on about it. Scott was so tired of having the same conversation. Jamie could do no wrong in their father's eyes. Perfect Jamie with his amazing degree, high-flying job, and equally perfect fiancée. Why couldn't Scott have had an older brother who was a fuck-up?

Just a few more months and then you're out of here.

Even if he didn't get the grades he needed for uni, he'd be leaving somehow. He'd get a job, any job, and find somewhere else to live. He needed to get out.

Once dinner was over, he helped clear up and then escaped to the sanctuary of his room. There was a message on his phone from Amy.

I miss you already xxx

Scott sighed heavily, feeling like the walls were closing in around him.

Miss you too, he replied, because that was what she'd be expecting to hear. Actually, he was quite happy to be alone this evening. Amy was okay; he didn't *mind* spending time with her. But he was never sad to say goodbye. He sighed. He should probably finish things with her soon. It wasn't fair to string her along when, yet again, he wasn't feeling any of the things he should be feeling for the girls he went out with.

When his phone buzzed again, he ignored it and got out his Biology paper. He lost himself in that until he started to yawn, and when he checked the time, he saw he'd done more than the two hours he'd promised his dad. Knackered then, he got ready for bed and settled down, waiting for sleep to come.

Despite his exhaustion, Scott's brain wouldn't switch off. He kept going over the incident with Olly from earlier. In the darkness with no distractions, he was plagued by the mental image of Olly flying off his bike because of Scott's carelessness. It replayed on a loop in his head. He hoped Olly wasn't too badly hurt. He must be pretty bruised from landing on the tarmac.

Scott got his phone from the bedside table and scrolled through to Olly's number.

They'd both got phones when they started at Fairfield, and after that they used to text each other random shit all the time until they ran out of their free texts for the month. Scott smiled at the memory, an ache in his chest.

Olly might have changed his number, but Scott typed a message anyway, hoping it would get through.

I'm really sorry about earlier. Are you okay?

He waited for a few minutes, but there was no reply.

With a heavy sigh, he put his phone aside and then tossed and turned for a long time. Finally he fell into a restless sleep, filled with weird dreams of overgrown gardens, black cats, and the scent of long, hot summers.

CHAPTER TWO

The sound of music playing pulled Scott from a thick blanket of sleep into wakefulness. He lay curled on his side; his room was darker than usual, as though someone had come in and closed the blinds while he slept. His bed felt weird, softer than it should be, and it smelled different.

He sat up, blinking in confusion as he looked around. He took in the room, the details unclear in the half-light that crept around the edges of the blind, but it was enough for him to realise where he was.

The posters on the wall were new, but the layout hadn't changed in four years.

What the fuck?

It wasn't possible. Logic told Scott there was no way this could be happening. He'd gone to sleep in his own bed—he hadn't been drunk or high. So why the hell was he waking up in Olly's room with no recollection of how he got there? And where the hell was Olly? The music that had woken him was coming from a phone on a docking station by the bed. He picked it up and pressed some buttons until it stopped. His brain was fogged with sleep and he couldn't think clearly.

Scott got out of bed on shaky legs. His hip ached as though it was bruised. Actually, his whole body felt weird. Perhaps he was sick? Maybe this was all some bizarre hallucination?

21

Pulling the cord to raise the blind, Scott flooded the room with light. He looked down at himself, only….

He closed his eyes and shook his head. When he opened them again, he still didn't see himself. His body was too thin, his skin too pale, the hair on his legs darker than usual, and he *definitely* didn't own any snug purple briefs like the ones he was currently wearing.

Stomach roiling with disbelief and terror, Scott turned to the full-length mirror on the wall and blinked.

Olly's reflection stared back looking as horrified as Scott felt. Scott raised his hands to his face, and so did Olly in the mirror.

"This isn't happening," he said.

The voice was Olly's too, softer and a little higher-pitched than Scott's own.

It was the weirdest, most vivid dream Scott had ever had.

He pinched himself hard. "Ouch!"

Why wasn't he waking up?

Beep beep beep beep beep beep beep!

Olly shot up, heart pounding at the shrill sound. He opened his eyes and blinked in the sunlight.

Ugh. Too bright.

He looked around wildly and closed his eyes again, refusing to believe what he saw. Obviously he wasn't awake yet because he couldn't be in Scott's room. He hadn't set foot in Scott's house in years.

Olly cracked his eyes open again but still saw the white walls, the posters of Scott's football heroes that Olly remembered from years ago, and the freakishly tidy desk that definitely wasn't his.

22

The alarm clock by the bed was still making an awful racket, so he found the button to silence it.

"Scott?" he said hesitantly, then coughed.

What the fuck was wrong with his throat? His voice was deep and rough sounding. *Oh God, no, please don't let me be getting a cold.* He couldn't afford to lose his voice with all the play rehearsals coming up.

He pushed the duvet off and swung his legs around to get out of bed. He'd find Scott and work out what the hell was going on. Maybe he had some weird amnesia after his accident yesterday, although he hadn't hit his head. There had to be some explanation for why he was apparently in Scott's bed rather than his own.

Then Olly looked down at his legs—and froze.

They were thicker and more muscular than they should be. Olly only dreamed of having legs like that. The hairs on them were light brown instead of dark, the skin more tanned. He looked at his hands, they were all wrong too, thicker and sturdier than they should be. He lifted one to run it through his hair, the way he often did in times of crisis.

"What the fuck?" No long floppy fringe falling in his eyes. Instead he found short-cropped hair and his ear piercings were gone.

Now convinced he was dreaming, because that was the only possible explanation, Olly got up to look in the mirror. Scott's handsome face stared back at him, the mouth slack with surprise and the blue eyes wide.

Olly shook his head in disbelief. No way could this be happening. *No way.* This was the stuff of Hollywood movies, not reality. But cold, creeping panic rose in his gut, because apart from the fact that he appeared to be in the wrong body, everything else felt normal. Way too normal for it to be a dream.

23

"No," he said loudly, putting his hands up and touching Scott's nose, Scott's cheekbones, Scott's lips. He felt every brush of his fingertips. "Oh, Jesus Christ on a bike, this is not happening. *No.*"

Galvanised by fear, Olly pulled on the first clothes he found, lying on the back of a chair, and shoved his feet into a pair of trainers. A glance at the clock told him it was half seven. If he was going to school today, he'd need to leave in less than an hour.

"Think, *think*! You need to focus," he muttered.

Taking a few slow, deep breaths helped clear his mind. He picked up Scott's school bag and let himself quietly out of the room.

He could hear someone in the kitchen as he crept down the stairs, and when he reached the front door, Scott's mum called, "Scott, is that you? Aren't you having any breakfast?"

"Not hungry!" Olly called back. "Sorry, I've got to rush. I've got a, um, thing at school I need to do. See you later!"

And he was out of the door, slamming it behind him before she could emerge from the kitchen.

He ran down the road to his own house, feet pounding on the pavement.

Knocking on his own front door was weird, but not half as weird as seeing the expression of surprise on his thirteen-year-old sister's face when she opened the door.

"What do you want?" She frowned at him, arms folded like a miniature bouncer.

"Oh. Hi, Sophie. I, uh, I need to see Sc—Olly. I need to see Olly urgently. Is he in?"

She rolled her eyes. "Where else is he going to be at half seven in the morning?"

24

"Sophie? What's going on, who is it?" Olly's mum came down the stairs, wearing her dressing gown.

"It's Scott. He's looking for Olly."

"Oh." Olly's mum gave him a searching look.

Olly pasted on what he hoped was a winning smile. "I'm really sorry to turn up so early, but it's important. I need to ask him something about a Biology... project thing." He waved his hand vaguely. Thank God he and Scott had one subject in common, otherwise he would have had no excuse to turn up on his doorstep. They hadn't hung out together in years.

"Well, okay. Let him in, Sophie."

Sophie stood aside, but she still looked suspicious. "You and Olly never normally even talk to each other."

Olly ignored her.

"Go on up, Scott," Olly's mum said.

As Olly passed his mum, he forced down the urge to tell her everything. She was his mum; she was supposed to make everything okay. But he didn't think his mum had the power to fix *this*.

Olly paused on the landing outside his bedroom. His heart pounded against his ribs and his hand shook as he lifted it to knock. If his hunch was wrong, who was going to be inside?

"Who is it?" Hearing his own voice through the door was totally bizarre.

Instead of answering, Olly opened the door and walked in, then closed it behind him.

He stared at the boy in the room. His own face looked back at him, green eyes wide and fearful.

"Scott?" Olly whispered. "Is that you?"

The Olly in front of him nodded. It was Scott, then. Good to know. At least it was only the two of them involved and not some freaky universal body-swap epidemic.

Then Scott added, "Are you Olly?"

Olly nodded. "Yeah, it's me. What the fuck's going on?" He wasn't expecting Scott to have an answer.

They sat on the edge of Olly's bed.

"Shit, shit, shit," Scott kept saying. His hands were shaking. "How is this possible? This can't be happening. What are we going to do?"

Somehow Scott's panic gave Olly the strength to stay calm. He clenched his—Scott's—fists, breathing slowly as his mind sorted through their options.

Scott carried on rambling. "Maybe we're both sick. Maybe someone gave us drugs? We have to tell our parents, Olly. I think we need to go to hospital." He seemed on the verge of hyperventilating.

"No," Olly said sharply. "We can't tell anyone about this."

Scott raised his head. "What? Why not? They might be able to help us!"

Tears shone in his eyes. It was so weird for Olly to see what he looked like when he cried. He was actually quite cute when he cried. Maybe he should do it more often.

Focus, Olly. Priorities.

"Seriously, Scott. Do you feel ill? Have you ever heard of an illness or drugs that can do *this* to a person? To two people?" He gestured between them.

Scott shook his head mutely, dark hair falling into his eyes.

26

Olly's fingers itched with the urge to brush it aside for him. "Think about it rationally for a minute. If we tell our parents we've... what? Swapped bodies or brains or whatever's happened here, do you think they're seriously going to believe us? They'll think we're crazy—like 'mentally ill, admitted to the psych ward' levels of crazy. We'll be locked up before the end of the day, and God knows what would happen to us then."

"So what do you suggest? What are we going to *do*, Olly?"

Scott sounded so helpless. It reminded Olly of when they got into trouble when they were kids. Scott had always been useless in a crisis. It seemed that hadn't changed.

"We're going to do the best job we can of being each other for the day so that nobody suspects anything. Then we're going to go to bed and hope everything's back to normal tomorrow. Okay?"

"Okay. Yes." Scott looked hopeful. "Maybe that's all we need to do—sleep again. This happened overnight, so it makes sense that we'll change back while we're sleeping."

Olly breathed a sigh of relief that Scott was on board with his plan. It might be weak, but it was the only plan they had. At least Scott had stopped freaking out.

"So let's do it. Now put some clothes on, for Christ's sake. It's weird seeing myself half-naked, and you need to hurry, or we'll be late."

Scott stood and looked down at himself. Olly noticed the scrape on his knee from the accident yesterday. A large bruise was forming around it. He winced. That must hurt this morning.

"This whole thing is weird," Scott said, running his hands thoughtfully over his chest and stomach.

Olly shivered, imagining the touch. "Stop feeling me up!"

Scott flushed, the stain of red spreading down his neck to his chest.

Wow. Olly had no idea it was so obvious when he was embarrassed. Good to know—*not*.

Thankfully his words had the desired effect, and Scott stopped touching himself like a weirdo, then asked, "What clothes should I wear?" He looked disapprovingly at Olly's floordrobe, which had reached epic proportions in the last week or so. "Jesus, Olly. Don't you ever pick up your clothes when you take them off?"

"I've been too busy learning lines for the play and revising," Olly said. "But there are clean ones in the drawers—second one down."

Scott picked out a T-shirt and pulled it on. It was a boring blue one, not one of Olly's favourites, but it would do.

"Jeans?" Scott asked.

Olly grabbed his second-favourite pair from the pile on the floor and threw them at Scott, who caught them.

"Seriously?" Scott wriggled into them, grimacing. "They're like a bloody straightjacket for my dick."

"Seeing as you fucked over my new pair yesterday by driving like a twat, you're stuck with these ones. Anyway, I think you'll find it's *my* dick. And they make my arse look awesome."

28

It was Olly's turn to flush. He hadn't had time to think about *that* aspect of being in someone else's body until now. The idea that Scott's genitals were literally his for the day took his mind to places they really didn't have time for. Maybe he could give it some thought later.

Scott was pink again, so maybe his mind had gone there too, although presumably not for the same reasons Olly's had. Well, at some point during the day, Scott was going to have to deal with touching Olly's dick. Because there was no way he'd get through twenty-four hours without peeing.

Speaking of which….

Olly stood. "I'm going to use the bathroom."

Scott snapped his head up, eyes wide. "Oh. Um… okay."

Olly rolled his eyes. "You finish getting dressed. Wear my Converse—the black ones—and the dark green hoodie on the back of the door. I'll be back in a minute."

He let himself out and crossed the landing to the bathroom.

His bladder was uncomfortably full, and as he unzipped and freed himself from Scott's boring black boxer briefs, his only focus was on relieving the pressure. He sighed in satisfaction as he let go and urine hit the water in the toilet bowl.

It felt good, like it always did.

Of course he couldn't help looking. I mean… who wouldn't, given a chance? Even if he hadn't been gay and didn't still have a shameful secret crush on Scott, he'd still have wanted to get a good look at his dick.

I'll show you mine if you show me yours.

They'd done that as kids, looking at the similarities and differences. They'd had competitions in the woods at the edge of the park to see who could pee the highest or the farthest. When they hit puberty, that had all stopped, and Olly was intrigued to see what Scott's penis looked like now. It was thick and fleshy in his hand, a little shorter and fatter than his was when it was soft. He'd pulled the foreskin back to piss, and when he finished, he shook out the last few drops and rolled the foreskin back over the head. The stroke of his fingers sent a little tingle through him.

I wonder what he looks like when he's hard?

That was kind of a creepy thought and Scott would notice if Olly took too long, so he resisted the urge to find out. He put it away, flushed the toilet, and washed his hands.

When he got back to his room, Scott was looking at him suspiciously.

"Oh, relax," Olly said airily. "Your virtue is safe."

"I need to go too."

"Have at it." Olly gestured to the door. When Scott returned, Olly's stomach growled. "God, I'm starving already. Normally I skip breakfast if I'm late, and I'm never hungry till break."

Scott shrugged. "I have a fast metabolism. Sorry. It's all the training."

"I'd better eat something here before we go, then."

"Won't your mum think it's weird? You can't go helping yourself to stuff in the kitchen looking like me."

"Not if you come with me," Olly said. "My mum's very chilled. It'll be fine."

30

When they went in, Olly's mum was sitting at the kitchen table, with a steaming cup of coffee. The affectionate smile she gave Scott made Olly's heart tug a little. Her expression was cooler as she studied him.

Olly waited for Scott to say or do something, but he was struck dumb, staring at Olly's mum like a rabbit in headlights.

"Hi, um… Mrs Harper," Olly said. "I didn't have time to eat before I came over, so Olly said I could have some cereal here. I hope that's okay?"

"Of course, Scott. Olly will show you where everything is."

Thankfully, she turned back to the magazine she was reading and her attention was diverted.

Scott looked at Olly and raised his eyebrows. Olly jerked his head at the fridge; boxes of cereal were lined up on top of it.

Scott went and got some muesli and bran flakes.

Olly tried not to make a face, but eww. He only ever ate cereal that involved massive amounts of sugar. Of course, Scott with all his football training and superhealthy ways probably never ate anything decent like Frosties or Honey Loops.

Scott opened a cupboard door at random, presumably looking for a bowl, and closed it again quickly when he realised it was full of pots and pans.

Olly surreptitiously pointed at the right cupboard and Scott took out two bowls.

Before Olly could signal his mistake, Scott filled both of them with an unappetising-looking mixture of the two cereals; then he got the milk out of the fridge and topped them up till they almost overflowed.

Scott hesitated again, and Olly realised he had no clue where to find a spoon. Again he pointed, and he thanked the universe that his mum wasn't paying attention to what they were doing.

Finally they sat at the table with their breakfast, and while Scott tucked in immediately with enthusiasm, Olly poked at his while his stomach rumbled unhappily.

"Nice to see you eating a healthy breakfast for once, darling," Olly's mum said.

Scott didn't react at first, so Olly kicked him sharply in the shin.

"Oh... uh. Yeah. It's kind of a new resolution."

"Well, that's great. I hope you stick to it."

Gee, thanks Scott.

Olly resisted the urge to kick him again—harder. Once he got his own body back, no way was he putting that horse food into it.

"Don't you like it, Scott?" Olly's mum gave a frown of concern. "You can have some toast instead if you want."

Olly didn't want to do anything to delay them leaving the house. They were already short on time, and he and Scott needed to work out a plan of action for the day. "No, really, this is fine. I was just waiting for the milk to sink in a little. I prefer it when it's more—" He poked it. *Soggy, disgusting.* "—when it's like this." Manfully, he scooped up a large spoonful and forced it down without chewing first, his gorge rising against the bland, lumpy mixture.

When he looked across the table at Scott, he was smirking at him. Damn him. Olly had perfected that smirk in front of the mirror. It was his trademark, and now it was being used against him.

Bastard.

32

The sooner they got their own bodies back, the better.

CHAPTER THREE

After breakfast, they went back up to Olly's room. Scott packed a bag with the stuff he needed for school—with Olly's help, of course, after checking his timetable. Everything required so much planning. It was only eight in the morning, and Scott was exhausted already.

"Right, we'd better head back to your house now. I need you to help me sort out what I need for today. Then I'll drive your car to school, obviously. And you can take my bike," Olly said.

Scott paused in what he was doing and frowned. "No way. You don't have a license."

"Oh, for crying out loud, I can drive as well as you. Better, if yesterday was anything to go by."

"I'm coming with you, then," Scott said stubbornly. He wasn't letting Olly loose in his wheels alone.

"But that will immediately make people suspicious. Everyone at school knows that I—" Olly winced. "—that *we* don't exactly get on."

That was an understatement. Olly had avoided Scott for years, and if he ever spoke to him, he said something cutting or dismissive.

Scott hated how much it still hurt, even after all this time. "Yeah, but we have the perfect excuse." He gestured down at his leg. "We can say your bike was damaged when I knocked you off it, so I had to give you a lift."

"I suppose." Olly frowned. "As long as you're suitably pissy with me, hopefully nobody will think it's weird. Do you think you can manage that?"

"I'm sure I can pull it off." Being pissed off with Olly wouldn't be too much of a challenge—he'd had plenty of practice. "Right. Let's go."

They said goodbye to Olly's mum. Scott was taken by surprise when she went in for a hug. His own parents weren't usually physically affectionate, so he felt rather awkward as she squeezed him.

"Bye, darling. Have a good day."

Scott patted her on the back and hoped she wouldn't notice anything unusual.

Back at his house, all was quiet. His dad usually left the house before anyone else was up, and his mum had gone to work by then too.

"Is there anything else I need for today?" Olly asked once they'd made sure he had the right books for Scott's lessons.

"Oh… yes." Horror dawned on Scott. "You need my football kit. I've got training after school. Shit. Do you even remember the rules? You haven't played for years."

Olly rolled his eyes. "Of course I remember. I was on the team in primary school. It's like riding a bicycle."

"Yeah… but the tactics are a little more subtle at this level."

"But the principle's the same. I'll cope. If I'm a bit crap, I'll tell the coach I'm feeling ill, or pretend to get cramp or something."

"Yeah, okay." Scott must have done a bad job of hiding his feelings, because Olly punched him in the arm.

35

"For fuck's sake, I'm not *that* bad at football. You should remember. We used to play together often enough. Anyway, I'm just going to have to do my best, aren't I, unless you want me to skip it?"

"No, you can't do that." Scott sighed. His coach was really strict about them attending all the practice sessions. With the finals coming up, he'd be in the shit if he slacked off now. He picked up his kitbag and gave it to Olly.

"Speaking of after-school activities," Olly said with a deepening frown, "you're going to have to go to the play rehearsals as me. Oh shit, Scott. That's going to be much harder for you to bluff your way through than football training."

Scott groaned. He hated anything that involved being on a stage in front of people. "When's the next rehearsal?"

"Tomorrow."

"Maybe we'll have changed back by then," Scott said hopefully.

"Maybe. But I'm not risking you fucking this up for me. We'll need to get together after school today and go through the script and blocking just in case. I'm supposed to know all the lines by heart now. I guess Miss Andrews might give me a little leeway if you plead homework and exam revision getting in the way of learning the script."

"What play is it?" Scott asked.

"Romeo and Juliet. And I'm Romeo, so there are loads of lines to learn."

Scott's day kept getting worse. "Okay," he sighed. "But let's get through today first, yeah?"

36

They argued the whole way to school. Despite Olly's criticism of Scott's driving, he was equally bad, in Scott's opinion.

"This car is awesome! You're so lucky," Olly said as he zoomed around a mini-roundabout way too fast, throwing Scott sideways into the door.

"Yeah. It is. The brake pedal is the one in the middle, by the way. Just in case you weren't aware."

Olly laughed unrepentantly and accelerated away.

By the time they reached school, Scott was a nervous wreck, and it wasn't even slightly hard to act furious with Olly.

"Thanks for the lift, arsehole." He slammed the door, and then remembered it was his own car and felt ridiculous.

"There's not actually anyone near us," Olly pointed out. "So you don't have to act like you hate me yet."

Scott just glared. "You make it really easy." Four years of hurt and resentment made it easy too.

Olly lowered his voice. "So. Plan for the day. Keep our heads down and try and act as normal as we can. Do you want a lift home too? I've got to go to your training session, of course, so I'll be leaving late."

"Yes. You're not driving my car without me in it. I'll go to the library. Come and find me when you're done."

"Good idea. You can start learning my lines while you're there. The book's in my bag. We'll be working on my first scene with Benvolio tomorrow, so you can start with that."

Olly locked the car, and Scott's fingers itched to take the keys from him.

"Oh, I just thought of something," Olly said. "We should give each other the passcodes for our phones. Then we can text each other during the day if anything comes up we need help with." He got Scott's phone out of his pocket and frowned at the lock screen. "Oh fuck. There are loads of missed texts from Amy while the sound was turned off. I think she's pissed off with you—which will be fun for me to deal with."

"Let me see." Scott grabbed the phone. Of course, his thumbprint wouldn't unlock it, so he quickly tapped in the code. He read the series of increasingly irate texts from Amy asking why he hadn't picked her up as he was supposed to that morning. "Oh bollocks. I totally forgot I'd promised to drive her to school this morning." He handed the phone back to Olly.

"Oh great," Olly said. "I guess that's my first mission of the day, then. Help me out here, Scott. I have no idea how to deal with angry girlfriends. Boyfriends are easy—there's nothing a blowjob can't fix."

Scott felt a lurch of discomfort at the thought. He pushed it away quickly. He didn't like to think about why he was jealous of Olly's boyfriends. Ever since Olly had come out at school a couple of years ago, Scott had hated it whenever Olly was dating anyone. "Text her to say sorry, make up a good excuse. Then buy her a chocolate chip cookie at break time and grovel a lot. That should do the trick."

"Will do." Olly got out a notepad and pen, and he jotted down his passcode for Scott, then tore out the page and gave it to him. "Now write yours down for me." He handed Scott the pad.

38

Scott's phone was already unlocked, and Olly was scrolling through things while Scott wrote down his lock code. Scott hoped Olly didn't find anything embarrassing.

Olly must be in his text messages because he said in surprise, "You tried to text me last night. I didn't get it, though, because my number's changed."

"Oh, yeah." Scott's cheeks heated. "I just wanted to check whether you were okay."

Olly's expression softened and he gave Scott a small smile. "That was nice of you, especially after I yelled so much."

Scott shrugged. "You had good reason."

Olly typed into Scott's phone. "There, I've put my new number in. Add yours to my phone."

"Mine hasn't changed."

"Yeah, but I deleted it ages ago."

Olly had the decency to blush, at least.

Scott wanted to ask Olly what he'd done to make Olly drop him as a friend. But now wasn't the time. They had more than enough to deal with today.

He added his number into Olly's phone and then put it in his pocket. Squaring his shoulders, he met Olly's gaze—his own blue eyes bored back into him.

"Right. Let's do this," Olly said with a grin. "It's kind of cool being you. I feel like a secret agent."

"I guess." Scott preferred life without the drama.

They walked together as far as the main entrance to the school and paused in the hallway. They were in different tutor groups now they were in the sixth form, so would be going their separate ways.

"Good luck," Scott said quietly.

"You too. See you later."

CHAPTER FOUR

Scott's phone buzzed in Olly's pocket as he walked down the corridor to find Scott's tutor group.

Olly paused to read the message. Amy again.

WHY AREN'T YOU REPLYING TO MY TEXTS?

So she'd graduated to shouty caps. Things were looking bad.

Deciding some damage limitation was in order before he had to see her face-to-face, Olly tried to channel Scott as he typed.

Really sorry. Accidentally left my phone turned off. Totally forgot lift. I'll make it up to you later. He added a few kisses afterwards, assuming Amy would be the sort of girl who'd appreciate that.

Her next message came back immediately.

You'd better, with an added angry-face emoji.

He ignored that and put the phone away.

As he walked along the corridor, he had to keep reminding himself that although he was Olly Harper on the inside, to the rest of the school he was Scott Morgan. It wasn't a huge school, so Olly knew everyone in the year, at least by sight. But blokes he normally never spoke to greeted him with grins and shouts of "Hey, Morgan. Alright, mate?" or "Scotty, how's it going?" and several girls fluttered their eyelashes at him and smiled coyly as he passed. He couldn't blame them—Scott was hot. But he ignored the girls; Scott was already in enough trouble with Amy.

Normally, Olly wouldn't care about saving Scott's arse, but seeing as he was the one dealing with the fallout today, he didn't want to do anything to make his life more difficult.

When he arrived at Scott's tutor room, a few other people were there, but no teacher yet. Olly paused uncertainly, then recognised one of the guys as someone Scott hung around with a lot: a tall boy with messy brown hair.

"Morning, Scott," he said with a smile.

Olly cast frantically around for the bloke's name. "Hi." He took the seat next to him, hoping that wasn't some social faux pas. God, it was hard trying to predict how Scott would act. Olly wished they were still friends, then at least he'd be more familiar with the details of Scott's life. He sneaked a look at the front of the bloke's planner: Martin Eades.

Oh yeah. Marty to his mates.

"How's things?" Marty asked.

"Not bad, thanks," Olly replied casually. "You?" He hoped to keep the conversation away from himself.

"Bored of revising. My parents are on my back 24/7. It's bad, man." Marty shook his head sorrowfully.

"Yeah, I know the feeling."

Actually, Olly didn't. His parents weren't the sort to put a load of pressure on him. Their view was that it was up to Olly. If he didn't get the grades, he didn't go to uni, and it was his life, not theirs. But he remembered enough about Scott's parents to assume they were probably more along the lines of Marty's. They'd always been really strict when Scott was younger, anyway. One time Scott's dad had grounded him for two weeks just because he got a bad grade in a maths test in Year 7. Olly hadn't known what to do with himself while the punishment lasted; he thought he was being penalised as much as Scott, because he missed him so much.

Olly pushed the memory away, uncomfortable with remembering those days when Scott had been the centre of his universe.

Just then, the teacher came in and started taking the register. Distracted by lingering thoughts of Scott, Olly forgot to answer Scott's name when it was called. He only realised when Marty kicked him and the rest of the class started laughing.

"Oh, sorry. Here, Miss."

"Not quite with us this morning, Scott?" She raised an eyebrow.

"Yeah. Something like that."

If only you knew.

Somehow, Olly got through a mind-numbingly boring double Economics lesson first thing. Seriously, why would anyone want to study that shit? Thankfully the teacher didn't call on him to answer any questions, so he was able to get away with taking notes that made no sense to him and pretending he was concentrating.

42

At morning break it was time to face Amy. She texted him as soon as the bell went at eleven.

Meet me in the Y13 area?

Remembering Scott's advice, Olly stopped to get a chocolate chip cookie from the snack bar on the way, and when he found her—sitting with Marty and a girl with red hair whom he thought was called Hazel—he presented it to her with the most winning smile he could muster.

"Hey, uh… sweetie, I bought you a cookie. I'm sorry about earlier. I had to give Olly a lift because I'd damaged his bike, and we were running late—"

"Sweetie?" Marty snorted, then tried to mask it with a cough as Hazel elbowed him.

Amy's perfectly groomed eyebrows disappeared behind her blonde fringe for a moment, but then her face broke into a soppy smile. "Aww, *sweetie*. That's cute. You should call me that all the time. And it's okay. Thanks for the cookie." She patted the empty seat beside her and leaned in to kiss him.

She tasted of bubblegum and fake-fruit lip gloss. Olly tried not to flinch away. *It's just like being in the play*, he told himself. *Imagine you're Romeo kissing Juliet.*

They hadn't rehearsed the kissing part yet, but Demi, the girl playing Juliet, was a friend of Olly's and way less intimidating than Amy.

Luckily the lure of the chocolate chip cookie won out and he escaped after a brief peck on the lips. But even that had been more than enough. If Olly hadn't already been sure girls did nothing for him, kissing Amy would have sealed the deal.

She fed him bites of cookie. Olly was quite happy about that. The cookie was delicious, and it kept her hands occupied. Once they were done, she sidled closer on the bench and put a proprietary hand on his thigh. She slid it higher, scratching over the denim with her perfectly manicured talons.

Olly shivered. Was this supposed to be sexy? Was Scott really into this—into her?

"Hey, Scotty," she murmured in his ear. "Can you come over to my place after school today? My mum's away at a conference, and my dad's working late."

Thanking the gods of extracurricular activities, Olly replied, "Sorry, I've got football training."

"You could come afterwards? I was hoping to pick up where we left off yesterday…."

"No, I can't," Olly said sharply, the thought of her and Scott together gave him an uncomfortable lurch of jealousy.

She blinked at him, the initial hurt on her face fast turning into a furious flush. "What's your problem?" she hissed.

Olly back-pedalled fast. "Sorry, sorry. I didn't mean it to come out like that. What I meant to say was I can't. I wish I could, honestly, sweetie, but I have studying to do. My parents won't let me out later if I'm already going to football training."

Her face softened again. "Oh, yeah. They're pretty strict, aren't they? Okay, that's a shame." She patted his thigh and started stroking it again. Olly covered her hand with his to stop it moving higher.

The bell rang signalling the end of break, and Olly was relieved to be able to get shot of Amy. Thankfully she did completely different subjects to Scott, so they didn't have any lessons together.

44

Of course, Olly had to hang out with Amy again at lunchtime, but at least having her as an anchor meant he didn't have to make any decisions about where to go or who to sit with.

The girl was seriously clingy, though.

Sitting in the cafeteria, Olly cast his gaze around looking for Scott. It took him a moment to remember he was actually looking for himself… and it was oddly difficult to recognise himself from this perspective, like seeing yourself on video. In reality he didn't look quite how he imagined.

Olly's mental image had got stuck somewhere around age fourteen before he had a late growth spurt. So he was looking for someone smaller and scrawnier, and it took a moment to spot Scott, in his body, standing with a group of Olly's friends at the sandwich bar.

Olly was still skinny, compared to Scott, anyway. Being in Scott's more muscular frame felt weird. But Olly wasn't that short anymore. Not far off average height, and lean and graceful-looking; he looked good, and his arse really was amazing in those jeans….

Realising he was reaching new levels of narcissism by checking himself out, Olly snorted, then covered his amusement with a cough as Amy looked at him curiously.

When her attention was drawn back to a conversation with Hazel, Olly raised his eyes to watch Scott again. Scott looked fairly relaxed, chatting to Demi. She laughed at something he'd just said, and nobody was looking suspicious.

After Olly had eaten, he gave Amy the slip by telling her he had to go and get a book from the library.

"I guess I'll see you tomorrow, then," she said with mournful eyes. "I'll miss you tonight."

"Um, yeah. Me too."

She took his hands and tugged him closer.

No way was he going to get away without a kiss. Taking control, he leaned in for a quick press of lips. "Gotta run." He tried to sound regretful. "Bye."

Hiding out in a quiet corner of the library, he texted his own number.

Hi, how's your day going? I don't think I've screwed your life up yet.

He pressed Send, then started typing again.

I need football info from you. What position do you play? Anything I should know about, anything to help convince them I'm you?

His stomach fluttered nervously at the thought. For all his bravado that morning, it had been years since Olly had done anything other than kick a football around in the park. He wasn't sure he could pull this off, but he knew how important it was to Scott to stay on the team.

Scott replied right at the end of lunch break.

I think I'm doing ok at being you. In footy I play right wing. Just be amazing and score loads of goals and nobody will know.

Olly snorted and replied.

No pressure then. It's a miracle your head fits through doorways. Okay, we've got biology next so I'll see you then.

46

At least in Biology, Olly knew where to sit because they were in the same class. Scott always sat one row back by the window, next to Marty. Olly sat at the back with Demi, and usually spent way too much time staring idly at the nape of Scott's neck and trying to forget how it had felt to kiss him.

He caught Scott's eye as he walked into the lab.

Scott gave him a fleeting glance, wary green eyes under Olly's dark fringe. He hadn't styled it right, there wasn't enough swept over to the side. Olly's fingers itched to go over there and fix it.

Damn Scott.

He took his seat next to Marty. Scott had been under Olly's skin for years. Olly had to suppress a snort of irony because now Scott was *literally* under his skin. God, this was so fucking weird. He pinched himself just in case there was any chance this was still a dream, after all, but no. The pinch hurt, and he didn't wake up.

Biology was a double period, taking them to the end of the school day. There was an awkward moment when Mr Brewster called on Olly to answer a question, and Olly answered as Scott before he remembered he wasn't supposed to.

Mr Brewster glared at him. "Really, Mr Morgan. Shouting out answers is the sort of thing I expect from my Year 7 classes, not my A level students."

Olly flushed as the rest of the class smirked at him. "I'm sorry, sir. I, uh, misheard the name."

Mr Brewster raised his eyebrows. "Because the names Oliver and Scott are so similar? I can see why you'd be confused."

Everyone laughed at that, and Olly's face felt hot enough to fry eggs on.

"Anyway, moving on…," Mr Brewster continued.

Olly sank lower in his chair, wishing it would swallow him.

CHAPTER FIVE

During football training, Olly was grateful for—and impressed by—the superior strength and speed of Scott's body compared to his own. Scott obviously looked after himself, and it showed in performance as well as appearance.

He missed a few passes at the beginning where he failed to anticipate the play, earning him some curses from his teammates and some yelling from Mr Buckley, the coach, from the sidelines, but he did better once he got his head into the game. Miraculously he got through the session without screwing anything up too badly—or so he thought. But the coach held him back at the end when the other boys headed for the showers.

"Scott, everything okay with you?" Mr Buckley asked. "You weren't yourself out there today."

Olly had to fight down the urge to laugh hysterically. *You could say that.* "Yeah. Sorry, Coach. Just revision stress messing with my head."

Mr Buckley frowned. "I know the exams are important, but it's only another couple of weeks till the season's over. Hold it together, yes? It's years since we've had such a good chance at winning the schools' county championship."

Olly nodded. "Yes, sir. I'll do my best. Sorry about today."

Mr Buckley clapped him on the back. "Good lad."

By the time Olly made it to the locker room, most of Scott's teammates were naked in the communal showers.

Not being part of any school sports teams, Olly wasn't used to showering with other people. He stripped off, trying not to look self-conscious, and made sure he kept his eyes up—even though the temptation to check out the other guys was strong.

Unsure how to interact with these people who were more-or-less strangers to him, he kept his mouth shut as the locker-room banter went on around him.

"You all right, mate?" Marty asked from beside him. "You're quiet today." Then he stuck his head under the showerhead and rinsed suds out of his hair.

Once his head emerged, Olly said, "Yeah, I'm okay. A bit tired, maybe."

Marty seemed to accept that as an excuse. "Did Mr Buckley give you a hard time?"

"No, not really. Just checking up on me."

"Yeah. He's a good bloke." Marty turned off the shower and slicked his hair out of his face. "See you in a few."

Olly was the last one left in the showers, and he soaped up quickly. The feeling of an alien body under his hands was totally freaky. He tried not to think about it too much as he ran his hands over the muscles of "his" chest and abs. Maybe if he went to the gym and ate more protein, he'd look like this in about ten years' time. He soaped his private parts quickly and didn't allow his hands to linger.

This was all so wrong. Talk about an invasion of privacy.

50

"How was football?" Scott asked as soon as they got in the car. He had a worried frown on his face.

"It was okay. Not your best practice, obviously. But it wasn't a disaster."

"What happened?"

"Nothing major. I fucked up a bit at the start, missed a few passes, but it got better. Coach had a word with me, and I claimed exam stress. He was cool about it."

Scott sighed heavily. "Okay."

"*Okay*? How about 'thanks'? I did my best for you. I even resisted the urge to check out your teammates in the shower, and believe me, that was hard. There are some hot guys on your team. The least you could do is be appropriately grateful."

"Yeah, sorry. Thanks—for trying, I mean." Scott flushed.

"How did you get on with learning the lines?" Olly asked as he turned the car out of the school car park.

"Ugh, I dunno. It's really hard to learn the words when they don't even make any sense. I've never understood Shakespeare."

"Shakespeare is awesome!" Olly protested. "Once you get used to it, you'll be fine."

Olly drove back to Scott's house and parked his car outside.

"Can we go back to yours to work on my lines?" Scott asked.

"Why not just stay here, seeing as we're here now?"

Scott shook his head. "No. My parents are funny about me having people over sometimes."

Olly knew Scott was being evasive, but he didn't push. "Okay, whatever. My folks won't care, and at my place we have decent snack food too."

They walked back to Olly's together, and as they approached, they saw Miss Wychwood in her front garden, kneeling and pulling up some weeds from a border. Beside her the black cat was lying in the sun, looking contented.

Miss Wychwood must have heard their footsteps on the pavement, because she looked up. Her gaze was piercing, and Olly felt uncomfortable with the level of scrutiny. Finally she smiled and he relaxed a little. "I'm glad you two have made up after yesterday."

"Yeah, hi." He nodded, without stopping.

Scott muttered a greeting too, clearly not keen to prolong the conversation either.

Olly got to the front door first and then realised Scott had his keys, so he got out of the way so Scott could open the door. "It sticks sometimes," he muttered. "Give the key a wiggle."

Nobody was in the kitchen when they got inside, so Olly took the chance to give Scott a quick tour of the kitchen while they gathered snacks to take up to his room.

"You should have done this for me when we dropped the car off at your place," Olly said.

"Yeah." Scott frowned. "It's too late now. My mum'll be home soon. I'll draw you a map of where things are instead."

"Good idea. Right, let's head up to my room."

On the landing they could hear pop music coming from Sophie's bedroom. The door to the spare room, which his parents used as an office, was ajar.

"Is that you, Olly?" his mum called.

"Yeah. Hi, Mum," Olly replied before he remembered he was in the wrong body. He clapped his hand over his mouth and looked in horror at Scott, who glared at him.

"Olly? Your voice sounds weird. Have you got a sore throat?" There was a sound of movement and she came to the doorway, frowning, but the sight of Scott distracted her. "Oh, you've got Scott with you. Hello again."

"Hi, Mrs Harper." Olly smiled winningly.

"We're going to work on this Biology project again," Scott said.

"Okay. Well, I've got work to finish, so I'll leave you to it."

Olly breathed a sigh of relief as she turned and went. How long was it going to take him to get used to answering to Scott instead of Olly? But hopefully they were going to wake up back in their normal bodies tomorrow, and this nightmare would be over.

They shut themselves in Olly's room and sat on his bed to run through lines. They got through most of act one. Scott wouldn't need all of it for tomorrow, only the first scene Olly was in, so he focused on trying to learn the words and direction for that. They'd worry about the rest of it another day if they had to. Luckily, Scott had a good memory for the lines and managed to pick up enough to get by with a little prompting.

The time flew by. They were so focused on trying to get Scott up to speed ready for tomorrow that they didn't notice how late it was.

It wasn't till Scott's phone buzzed with a text from his mum asking where he was that they realised it was half past six.

"Shit," Scott said. "She's going to be really pissy with you. I'm sorry. I should have kept an eye on the time. You'd better hurry."

Olly jumped up and grabbed his bag. "Yeah, okay. Do you want a lift in the morning again?"

"Let's wait and see what happens overnight. Maybe we'll be back to normal tomorrow."

"I bloody hope so. Today was the most stressful day ever. Okay, well. Let's text in the morning when we know what's going on."

Scott saw Olly out. On the doorstep, Olly asked quietly. "I forgot to check. What do you usually do in the evening? Just so I can… you know, be convincing as you."

"I hide out in my room and do homework, mostly revision and past papers at the moment. Amy sometimes texts or calls. Apart from dinner and helping to clear up after, I don't see much of my parents."

"Same," Olly said. "Okay. I'll see you tomorrow, whatever happens."

"Yeah. Good luck with my mum." The expression on Scott's face suggested Olly would need it.

Sure enough, as soon as he let himself in after fumbling a little with the unfamiliar lock, Mrs Morgan called through from the kitchen.

"Where have you been? You didn't tell me you were going to be late today."

54

Wow, given that Scott was eighteen, her concern seemed a bit excessive. She'd always been overprotective though. Olly remembered the time he'd been round playing at Scott's when they were about ten or eleven, and they'd gone to the park and come back ten minutes later than Mrs Morgan had said. She'd flipped out. Scott had been sent to his room, and Olly had been sent home.

As he entered the kitchen, Olly pasted on a shamefaced expression that he hoped was authentic. "I'm really sorry, Mum. I was studying at a friend's house and lost track of time."

Mr Morgan was there too. Stern and formidable in his suit, he looked at Olly over the top of his glasses.

"Which friend?" Mrs Morgan asked as she carried a bowl of salad to the table.

"I was with Olly."

His parents exchanged a quick glance. Olly thought that Mrs Morgan gave a slight shake of her head, but if she did, Mr Morgan ignored it.

"I didn't think you hung around with *him* anymore," Mr Morgan said. The emphasis on *him* was unmistakable and disapproving. It made Olly's skin crawl.

"We're working on a Biology project together." He stuck to the story they'd used with his mum. "It's not like I have much choice in the matter. The teacher allocated the pairings."

Scott's father was still frowning. "Hmm. Well, I suppose not. But just be careful about spending too much time with boys like that. You don't want people to get the wrong idea."

The shock left Olly gaping. "Boys like *what*?" he snapped before he could think better of it.

"Homosexuals, of course. You know my opinion on the matter."

Olly blinked and bit the inside of his cheek to stop himself arguing further. This wasn't his battle to fight, and he had no idea how Scott would respond in this situation. Shocked and stinging from Mr Morgan's words and obvious dislike of him when he hadn't done anything to deserve it other than be himself, Olly had no idea what to say.

Thankfully, Mrs Morgan rescued him. "Sit down, Scott. Dinner's ready." Points of colour showed in her cheeks and a frown tugged at her brow, but her voice was kind.

Olly sat, and Mrs Morgan dished up plates of supermarket lasagne. There was bread to go with it as well as the salad. Olly had been hungry, but the conversation with Mr Morgan had stolen his appetite, leaving him feeling sick and anxious. He picked at his food, forcing down as much as he could.

Olly didn't remember Mr Morgan much from when they were kids. He'd usually been working late, and they'd always spent more time at Olly's house or outdoors than here. But from the interactions he remembered, Mr Morgan had been perfectly pleasant to Olly when he was a kid.

Olly supposed that was before he'd gone through his nail-varnish-and-eyeliner stage at fifteen—not that any of that proved he was gay, but Mr Morgan seemed sure. Since Olly had come out at school at sixteen, it wasn't a secret. Everyone knew. He sometimes held hands with his boyfriends in the street or kissed them goodbye outside his house. Olly didn't hide his sexuality, and why should he?

Because of homophobic arseholes like Mr Morgan.

He sighed.

"Eat up," Mr Morgan barked. "Don't waste good food."

Olly forced down the rest of the lasagne. It wasn't nearly as nice as the homemade one his dad cooked.

After dinner, Olly was glad to escape upstairs. He closed Scott's bedroom door behind him and let out a long sigh of relief. Scott's parents hadn't batted an eyelid when he'd muttered something about revision and a project to finish. Olly had all the wrong books apart from Biology. He did some half-hearted studying for a couple of hours, and then Scott's phone buzzed with a text from Amy.

Hi baby, I'm bored and thinking of you xxx

Olly wondered how Scott would respond. He ended up going with the hopefully safe option of *Me too x*

Can we Skype?

Ugh. Olly was so done with pretending to be Scott. His brain needed a break from the effort.

I can't. My wifi's crap tonight.

He got back a row of sad faces and rolled his eyes. Apparently one wasn't enough to get her point across. He replied as Scott.

Sorry. I'll see you at school tomorrow.

Okay xxx

Thank goodness that seemed to be the end of it. Hopefully, by tomorrow, Olly would be back in his own body and Scott could deal with Amy again.

He went back to revising, but by ten o'clock he was yawning. It was mentally exhausting being someone else for the day, and his—that is, Scott's—body was knackered from football training.

Olly went to the bathroom to piss and brush his teeth. He hadn't done them in the morning due to the stress of this situation. Luckily there was only one toothbrush in the bathroom to choose from, so that was easy. Scott's parents must have an en-suite in their room.

When he got back to Scott's bedroom, he stripped down to his boxers and T-shirt and got into Scott's bed. Olly turned off the light and settled down, hoping sleep would come quickly. But once he warmed up, he was too hot, so he took off his T-shirt too.

Lying on his back, he stared up into the darkness. With the scent of Scott all around him and the brush of sheets on his bare skin, Olly felt a prickle of heat gather in his groin and his—Scott's—dick stirred and began to harden.

"Oh no. No, no, *no*." Olly curled onto his side and drew his knees up, trying to ignore the now-insistent throbbing in his underwear. The mere thought of touching himself there, of finding out what Scott felt like when he was hard and how his body would respond only made Olly more turned on. But the fact that he wanted to do it for those reasons meant he couldn't. It would be creepy and wrong, and even though Scott would never know, Olly wouldn't be able to look him in the eye.

"I deserve a fucking medal for self-restraint," he muttered.

All those years of wanting to touch Scott, and now this. It was torture.

58

Forcing all thoughts of Scott and masturbation from his mind, Olly made himself think of horrible things—boils and warts and puke and stuff like that—until finally his erection subsided and he was able to go to sleep.

CHAPTER SIX

Scott woke early. As soon as he stretched, he knew he was still in Olly's bed. He could tell by the scent of Olly on the sheets and the lighter weight of the duvet compared to his own.

"Bollocks." His heart sank. Any hopes that they would miraculously switch back overnight were dashed.

He looked at the time on Olly's phone—only six thirty. Olly would probably still be asleep.

Scott yawned and stretched, wondering if he could doze off for another half hour or so. He still felt tired, so maybe…. But then he realised that although he was still sleepy, one part of him was definitely wide awake—a heavy, insistent weight in Olly's snug briefs that didn't feel like it would go away anytime soon.

Scott reached down to adjust the unwelcome erection and the touch of his hand felt good. Too good. *Dangerously* good.

Nope.

Maybe a cold shower would help.

He got up and pulled on a long T-shirt to cover the bulge and then crossed the landing to the bathroom.

It felt wrong even looking at himself while he was hard, but it rather drew the eye. Scott was impressed despite himself. If this were his dick, he'd be pretty proud of it. Olly might be on the short side in stature—well, compared to Scott—but he definitely wasn't short in dick size. It was a bit slimmer than Scott's, but a good inch longer. It got even harder as he stared at it, curving up towards him. If dicks could look hopeful, then this one was practically giving him puppy eyes.

Down, boy.

Stepping into the shower, Scott turned it on full blast as cold as it would go. Even the most determined erection couldn't compete with that for long, and in a minute or so it had shrivelled and Scott was safe from temptation.

When he got back to Olly's room, Olly had texted.

No change here. Same for you I assume?

Scott replied. *Yeah.*

This sucks. I'll pick you up in half an hour so we can talk before school.

Okay.

Scott took off the towel around his waist and stepped into a clean pair of Olly's underwear before his dick got any more ideas. He wriggled into the same jeans as yesterday and rummaged in Olly's drawers until he found a T-shirt that he remembered Olly wearing around school.

Downstairs in the kitchen, he found Olly's parents and Sophie bustling around getting in each other's way as they made whatever combination of toast, cereal, tea, or coffee they were having.

"Morning." Scott tried to appear casual, but his stomach lurched with anxiety. He was worried he'd give himself away by saying the wrong thing or doing something stupid.

They greeted him casually and went back to what they were doing. Nobody seemed to pay him much attention, which was a relief.

Scott managed to remember where most things were and helped himself to some cereal. There was an awkward moment when he opened the wrong drawer looking for cutlery, but nobody noticed, so he closed it quickly and got the right one on his second try.

By the time he sat down at the kitchen table, the rest of them were there eating. Mr Harper was reading a magazine, and Sophie was glued to an iPod with headphones in as she stared at a YouTube video.

Mrs Harper looked up at Scott and smiled. "Did you sleep well, love?"

"Yes, thanks." He had actually slept surprisingly well given the situation. Olly's bed was comfortable, and yesterday had been exhausting.

"It's nice to see you spending time with Scott again." But something in her expression made Scott unsure how genuine her words were. A tiny crease formed between her eyebrows. "You used to be such good friends when you were younger."

"Yeah," Scott said noncommittally.

"Just…." She studied him and lowered her voice a little as she continued. "Just be careful, okay? I'd hate to see you get hurt again."

Scott blinked at her. What did she mean? Olly hadn't been hurt. He'd been the one to dump Scott as a friend. If anyone had been hurt by the breakdown of their friendship, it was Scott. But he couldn't ask her to explain, so instead he gave a small shrug. "It's fine, Mum. Don't worry."

"I'm your mother. It's my job to worry about you." But she smiled as she said it, and the tension lifted.

After breakfast, Scott kept turning her words over in his head as he brushed his teeth and packed Olly's school bag. What had Olly told his mum to make her think he had been upset?

The sound of a car horn outside drew him out of his musings. Scott ran downstairs, shouting out a goodbye to Mrs Harper, who was in her office.

Olly greeted him with a wan smile. "Hey," he said as Scott strapped himself into the passenger seat. "Amy wants a lift to school, but we need to talk first."

"Okay."

As they pulled away, Scott glanced out of the window and thought he saw the curtains move in the front window of Miss Wychwood's house.

Olly pulled up a few streets away, next to the park they used to play in when they were younger.

He turned to look at Scott and gave a heavy sigh. "So. Not just a twenty-four-hour aberration, then."

Scott sighed. "I guess not."

"What do you think caused it?"

Scott's mind went back to the flicker of movement from Miss Wychwood's front windows, and he frowned. Maybe it was a crazy theory, but it wasn't much crazier than their reality. "This might sound weird. But do you think it could be anything to do with Miss Wychwood?"

He bit his lip and watched a frown spread over Olly's face. Olly didn't reject his theory outright, and the furrow in his brow deepened.

"It happened after she saw us arguing," Olly said thoughtfully. "And she said something weird… about fate or something? But how could she make this happen? It's impossible."

"But it *has* happened." Scott shrugged. "Look at us."

"Should we talk to her? Find out why she's done it, and how we change back?"

"I don't know if that's a good idea. What if we're wrong? She'd think we were mad. She might tell our parents we were hassling her."

"Oh shit. Yeah. Maybe not, then." Olly sighed. "But whatever's going on here, it must have happened for a reason. When stuff like this happens in movies, it's because there's something that needs to be fixed. Something that needs to be sorted out by the people involved."

Scott thought back to what had happened the day before yesterday. What had Miss Wychwood said to them? Something about how they used to be best friends… but weren't anymore.

This isn't how it's supposed to be.

"Maybe we need to be friends again," he suggested.

Olly snorted. "Well, we spent some time together yesterday without bitching too much. So, why haven't we turned back?"

"I don't bloody know!" Scott heaved out a frustrated breath and banged his head back against the seat. "I guess one day of being civil wasn't enough. We've got four years to make up for."

Maybe it would help if he understood better how things had gone wrong between them, and the only way to make sense of that was to ask Olly about it, but they didn't have time for a lengthy discussion now. "We'd better go and get Amy. Let's focus on getting through another day, then maybe we can get together again this evening and see if we can work out what's going on and whether we can do anything to fix it."

"Okay." Olly started the engine. "You'll need to direct me to Amy's."

Amy came out of her front door as soon as Olly pulled up outside. Her smile faded when she saw who was in the passenger seat. Scott gave her a half-arsed smile and a wave, but she ignored him, going around to the driver's side and leaning in through the open window to greet Olly.

"Hi, baby." She ruffled his hair.

Olly immediately smoothed it back into place, and Scott tried not to smirk in satisfaction. Seeing her touching Olly, even in Scott's body, made him uncomfortable. He was glad Olly didn't seem to like it.

"Hi, Amy." Olly sounded convincingly pleased to see her.

She kissed him on the lips and Olly kissed her back. It wasn't even a passionate kiss, but something twisted in Scott's gut that felt like jealousy, and then he realised it was Amy he was frowning at rather than Olly, and that was as confusing as hell. Who was he actually jealous of?

Luckily the kiss was only a quick one, so Scott didn't have too long to ponder his unexpected reaction.

"I'll get in the back, then."

Amy glared pointedly at Scott, but he didn't offer to move. She had an annoying habit of groping him when he was driving, and he didn't want her distracting Olly while he was behind the wheel of Scott's pride and joy.

She climbed in on a waft of floral body spray. "Is your bike still broken, then, Olly? It didn't look that bad to me."

"Yeah, well, you're not really an expert, are you?" Scott said shortly, surprising himself at how easy it was to snap at Amy.

He felt guilty immediately. She wasn't a horrible person. It wasn't her fault that he didn't like her enough.

Olly glanced sideways and seemed to be fighting back a smile.

"Whatever." Amy sniffed.

When they got to school, she took Olly's hand as soon as they got out of the car. "Come on, let's go." She tried to tug him away from Scott.

"I'll see you later, then, Scott," Scott said. It was so odd saying his own name. "Shall I come to your house again this evening, like yesterday?"

"What?" Amy dropped Olly's hand and wheeled around to face him, hands on her hips and a frown on her pretty brow. "You were at *his* house last night? But you told me you couldn't come around to mine because you had to study!"

"Uh, yeah. But I was studying. We were working on a project together, so my parents made an exception and let me go round there," Olly said quickly.

"What project?"

"Something for Biology."

She raised her eyebrows. "Isobel didn't mention any Biology project."

Scott winced. Isobel was one of Amy's BFFs, and she was in the same Biology class as Scott and Olly. This was going to get ugly fast. "It was more of a revision thing," he chipped in. "I was stuck on something and O—*Scott* helped me out."

Amy gave up arguing, but her expression remained unconvinced and more than a little pouty.

"Come on, sweetie." Olly put his arm around Amy's shoulders. "Let's go. I missed you last night, and we've got ten minutes till registration, so let's make the most of it."

Scott fought back the urge to roll his eyes.

Sweetie? What the fuck?

He'd never called a girl *sweetie* in his life. He watched Amy and Olly as they walked away, arms around each other, and tried not to imagine how Olly would keep her happy for the next ten minutes. If Scott knew Amy, it would involve a public display of affection. She liked everyone to know they were together.

During registration, Olly's phone buzzed in Scott's pocket. He pulled it out surreptitiously to read the message from his own number.

I just had to snog your girlfriend up against her locker for FIVE WHOLE MINUTES. But she's forgiven me/you/us now. You owe me big time. That was not fun for me, just to be clear.

Scott knew he should be grateful to Olly for doing what he thought Scott wanted. But he couldn't help wishing Amy had been so pissed off that she dumped him. That would make everything a lot simpler.

The thought persisted through English Lit class. Scott's mind kept coming back to it when he was supposed to be making notes on Dickens's *Great Expectations*. If Amy did break up with him, would he care at all? After ruminating on it until the end of first period, he decided that no, he would honestly be relieved.

If only he was in a position to do it himself, he'd finish with her—the sooner the better now he knew it was the right thing to do.

At break time, Scott went with Demi to the cafeteria, where they met Olly's other friends from drama club. After hanging out with them yesterday, Scott was already pretty comfortable with them. They were a nice crowd, fun and quirky, and it was easy to relax in their company. Scott felt a pang of envy for Olly.

With his mates from football, Scott had to be constantly on guard. They were decent enough blokes, but there was a lot of macho bullshit and they were always putting each other down—in a jokey way, but one that kept Scott on edge. In Olly's crowd, nobody called anyone else *gay* in a disparaging way. It was refreshing.

Scott caught sight of Olly on the other side of the room, with Marty and the other lads Scott usually hung out with. He winced as he imagined Olly being part of that banter, and hearing *gay* used as an insult. He hoped Olly would know Scott didn't say that stuff. Scott never had, and he never would, but he was suddenly ashamed for not challenging his friends when they did it. He vowed that when he got back into his own body, that was going to change.

As he watched, Amy approached them and sat in Olly's lap. Olly reached up and brushed her hair out of her face in a casual gesture of intimacy. Scott's gut clenched and he looked away quickly, confused again by his reaction, but not wanting to think too hard about it. He had enough to worry about already.

The rest of the school day passed uneventfully. Scott managed to get through Olly's lessons without giving away his complete lack of knowledge. Fortunately they were at the time of the year where they were mostly going through past exam papers and example questions, so there was a lot of listening and note-taking and not too much discussion.

At lunchtime he sneaked off to the library to go through the lines for the rehearsal after school. Thank God he had a good memory, because he reckoned he knew them well enough not to raise suspicion. He wasn't word perfect, but he'd get by with a prompter.

After double Psychology in the afternoon, Scott decided Psychology was awesome. He'd wanted to take Psych A level, but his dad had told him it was a soft option and convinced him to go with Economics and Business Studies instead, a decision Scott later regretted. His dad had been very disappointed when Scott applied to study Biology at uni rather than something business related, but by then, Scott was done letting his father tell him what to do.

When the bell rang to signal the end of school, Scott's stomach lurched with anxiety and his palms started to sweat. He hadn't been in a school play since he was Joseph in the school nativity when he was seven years old. The thought of having to act, even just in front of the rest of the cast of the play, made him feel physically sick. For a panicky moment, he wondered whether he could claim illness and duck out of it. But Olly had gone to football training for him yesterday, and he'd done his best for Scott. Scott owed him the same courtesy.

Squaring his shoulders, he strode off towards the drama hall.

Once more unto the breach... or something like that.

Rehearsal went surprisingly well. Scott fluffed a lot of lines and needed prompting more than anyone else, but Miss Andrews, the director, seemed to accept his apologies and claims of putting revision first.

"As long as you know them by the dress rehearsal, Olly. But it's less than two weeks now."

"I'll do it, I promise," Scott assured her. Hopefully by then it would be Olly's problem, not his.

Once Scott got over his initial nerves, he was surprised to find he even started enjoying himself. Playing the part of someone else was rather liberating—although it was easier when you had a script. Having to improvise while pretending to be Olly was way harder than being Romeo with his lines decided for him.

When the rehearsal was over, the cast dispersed quickly, eager to get home. Scott was putting his script away in Olly's bag when a boy in the year below him—Marcus, who was playing Mercutio—came over to him.

"You were really good today," Marcus said in a low, intimate voice that grabbed Scott's attention.

Scott jerked his head up, realising they were alone and Marcus was standing close to him. Far closer than any straight boy ever would. Marcus's gaze dropped to Scott's mouth and he licked his lips.

Oh.

"Um, thanks," Scott replied nervously.

"Mercutio's a great role," Marcus said. "But if they let boys play the female parts, like they did in Shakespeare's day, I'd have auditioned for Juliet instead. Especially if I'd known *you* were going to be Romeo."

Scott realised he was frozen to the spot. Unsure of how to react, he was afraid of blowing his cover. He tried to imagine how Olly would behave. Scott might not be used to boys flirting with him, but he was pretty sure Olly was. Olly had had a few boyfriends since he'd come out and obviously wasn't inexperienced.

Trying to channel Olly, Scott forced a smile and turned towards Marcus. He studied him. Scott didn't usually let himself think too much about what other guys looked like, but Marcus was attractive. He actually looked a little similar to Olly. Same height, same lean body, but his hair was dirty blond and a little wavy where Olly's was dark and perfectly straight. Marcus's lips were soft and parted, damp where he'd licked them.

"Yeah?" Scott said slowly, hoping he sounded sexy rather than freaked out as his voice came out a little rough.

"Yeah." Marcus sidled closer. "Kissing you would be awesome."

"Even with an audience?" Scott tried to keep his voice light.

Marcus chuckled. "That part might be weird, but we don't have an audience now." He reached out, hooked a finger in Scott's belt loop, and tugged.

Scott resisted for a moment, but then he remembered that as far as everyone else in the world was concerned, he wasn't Scott. He was Olly. Everyone knew Olly was gay. Scott could kiss Marcus, and nobody would think it was weird, or wrong… and maybe it would help him answer a question that had been niggling away at the back of his brain for the last four years. Ever since the first—and only—time he'd kissed another boy.

With that thought, Scott capitulated. Committing to the role, he closed the gap between them and pressed his lips to Marcus's. Marcus responded immediately, opening his mouth to deepen the kiss and putting his hand on Scott's hips to keep him close.

It was a good kiss. Somehow very different to kissing Amy or any of the other girls he'd snogged. Inevitably, Scott's mind went to the other boy he'd done this with.

He closed his eyes and thought of Olly, remembered the darkness of the tent, the sweetness of the moment, and the terrifying arousal he'd been utterly unprepared for. His body reacted, whether to the memory of kissing Olly or to what was happening now, he wasn't sure.

Marcus moaned into the kiss and pressed closer, and Scott could tell he was getting hard too.

He was about to break the kiss and back away, when he heard a shocked voice say, "Scott?"

Scott jumped away from Marcus as though his lips were on fire. Olly was standing and staring at them. His expression was hard to read.

"Oh. Um… hi," Scott glanced sidelong at Marcus, who was frowning at Olly.

"Did you just say 'Scott'?" Marcus asked. "I thought *you* were called Scott."

"No. You must have misheard. I said let's go." Olly jerked his head towards the door. "Sorry to break up this little party, but I'm giving Olly a lift home and I'm in kind of a hurry. Come on, *Olly*." His voice dripped with sarcasm.

It was only when Scott heard that tone directed at him again that he realised how much nicer Olly had been to him since they'd swapped bodies.

Ugh. If they were supposed to be making friends in order to get back to normal, Scott suspected they'd taken several steps backwards in that department… but he wasn't sure why Olly was quite so pissed off.

"Okay," Scott said. "Bye, Marcus. See you soon."

Marcus gave him a soft smile but didn't make a move to kiss him again, and Scott was relieved. "Yeah, bye, Olly."

Scott picked up Olly's bag, slung it over his shoulder, and followed Olly, who was already stalking away.

"What the fuck was that?" Olly asked as soon as they were in the car. "Why the hell were you kissing Marcus?" He slammed the gears into reverse and backed out of the space way too quickly.

"I don't know," Scott said weakly. He honestly didn't know exactly. It had all happened so quickly. "He came on to me, and I didn't want him to realise anything was different, so I thought 'what would Olly do?'"

"And you obviously thought that Olly would just shove his tongue down some random's throat for no reason other than he could?" The wheels spun as Olly turned out onto the road and accelerated hard.

"For fuck's sake, slow down. And yeah, I guess so? I don't fucking *know*, okay. You've had lots of boyfriends, and Marcus seemed cute…. It was only a kiss, not a blowjob. Calm down."

Olly's eyebrows nearly hit his hairline. "Dear God, please tell me you're not considering giving anyone a blowjob. You'd be crap at it, and you'd ruin my reputation."

The thought of Olly giving blowjobs made Scott irrationally angry. "If you're dishing out enough blowjobs to *have* a reputation, why is it so bad that I snogged Marcus?"

"Because I've been saying no to him for weeks. He's way too keen, he's not my type, and now I won't be able to get rid of him."

Olly's jaw was still set and furious.

Scott wondered who was Olly's type, but it wasn't the right time to ask. "You can just tell him it was a mistake."

"No. *You* can tell him it was a mistake. You're the one who got me into this mess."

"Okay." Scott shrugged.

There was a long silence as they both focused on the road. Olly had stopped driving like a maniac now, at least.

Finally, as Olly turned the car into their street, he said, "You looked like you were enjoying it—for someone who isn't gay."

His voice was oddly tense, and Scott wasn't sure how to answer. He couldn't tell Olly that he enjoyed it because he was remembering the time *they'd* kissed, that during the kiss he'd been thinking about Olly rather than Marcus.

Before he could come up with a neutral response, Olly continued. "But I've been wrong about *that* before."

The bitterness in his tone made Scott's stomach twist.

The car lurched to a halt outside Olly's house.

"I'll see you after dinner, then?" Scott asked tentatively. "To go over more lines?"

"Yeah." Olly stared at his hands on the steering wheel, avoiding Scott's eyes. "See you later."

Scott couldn't help slamming the door behind him. Pissed off with Olly, pissed off with himself for unwittingly fucking things up, he was pissed off with everything.

Miss Wychwood's black cat was sitting on the garden wall, watching him.

"What are you looking at?" he muttered.

The cat stared, unblinking, until Scott turned away and stomped up the path to Olly's front door.

CHAPTER SEVEN

Olly went straight up to Scott's room and threw himself down on the bed. He glared at the ceiling as though it had personally offended him.

Seeing Scott kissing Marcus had burned Olly up with white-hot jealousy.

Olly was almost sure he was the only boy Scott had ever kissed—until today. And he'd wanted it to stay that way. The only way he'd been able to deal with Scott's rejection was through knowing it wasn't personal. It was just that Olly was the wrong sex.

Memories he'd pushed down and buried rose to the surface, sending tendrils through his brain and lighting up his senses. Over the years, Olly had tried so hard not to remember that night. The night when he'd had his heart broken and lost his best friend, all because of a kiss.

Olly squeezed his eyes shut, but that made it worse because images rushed in and the sense memories became even stronger. Scott looming over him in the darkness, the sticky summer heat of the tent, the sensation of Scott's lips on his….

Unable to hold the thoughts back, Olly gave up the fight and let himself remember.

Summer 2012

"What do you think it feels like to kiss someone?" Scott asked.

"Wet. Maybe a little slimy?" Olly suggested, trying to sound flippant.

He didn't want to have this conversation with Scott. Olly already spent far too much time thinking about his best friend in ways that made him feel guilty. He'd read on the Internet it was normal to have crushes on your friends sometimes; it didn't mean you were gay. But Olly was pretty sure it was more than a crush for him. His feelings for Scott were powerful and complicated and went beyond friendship. Sometimes he couldn't help hoping maybe Scott thought about him like that too.

Scott hadn't had a girlfriend yet, and it wasn't because of lack of opportunity. All the girls in their year fawned over him. Olly wasn't interested in girls at all, maybe Scott wasn't either?

Scott snorted. "Eww." There was a long pause. "But seriously, though. It must feel good, otherwise why would people do it?"

Olly didn't know how to answer. He shrugged, bumping shoulders with Scott where they lay side by side in the darkness. "I dunno."

It was a hot summer night, and they were camping out in a tent in Olly's garden. The night covered them like a blanket.

"Katie told me that Jennifer wants me to ask her out," Scott said quietly.

Olly's gut churned unpleasantly at the thought. "Are you gonna?"

"I don't know."

"Do you fancy her?" Olly couldn't help asking. It was like picking a scab. He dug a little deeper. "Do you want to kiss her?"

"I don't know. I can't imagine doing it. But she went out with that boy in Year 9 for ages, and they were always snogging by the lockers at school." Scott paused and sighed.

"So?"

"So if I ask her out, she's going to want me to do that too. And what if I'm crap at it? Snogging, I mean. I don't get what you're supposed to do with your tongue, or where to put your hands, or any of it really."

Olly's brain burned as he imagined Scott kissing Jennifer, the scene as vivid as if he'd taken a photograph of it. Scott's blond head and Jennifer's dark one, his hands on her face as tilted her head back. Olly thought he might die of jealousy if he actually had to witness it.

A crazy idea popped into his head. The darkness made him bold, and before he had time to chicken out, he blurted out his suggestion. "You should kiss me. I mean… we should kiss each other. To work out how to do it. That way we'll both know… for future reference. And if we're crap, it won't matter because neither of us are gonna tell anyone about it, are we? If we do it, I mean."

Olly finally stopped talking, his pulse pounding in his ears as he waited for Scott to react. Sweat prickled on his back and the heat of the summer night was suddenly oppressive.

"Wouldn't that be weird?" Scott finally asked.

"Probably. But who else are you going to practise snogging with? Unless you want to go in unprepared with Jennifer and take your chances."

Olly figured it was worth pushing him a bit. Scott hadn't said no outright and didn't sound shocked. Olly wasn't sure what he was doing, but now that the idea of kissing Scott had lodged in his brain like a splinter, he wasn't going to let it go too easily. This might be his only chance.

There was another long pause.

"Okay, then," Scott said.

"Okay then, what?" Hope flared, but Olly wanted to be 100 per cent sure.

"Let's do it. Let's try kissing."

"Now?" Olly's heart was beating so fast, he felt dizzy. Was it possible to have a heart attack when you were fourteen years old?

"Yeah. Come on." There was a rustle of movement as Scott rolled onto his side. It was too dark to see his features. "Do you want to put the lamp on?"

"No," Olly said quickly.

The darkness lent an intimacy, a false feeling of safety that might be chased away by the light.

Olly turned to face Scott. With their heads on two separate pillows, they weren't close enough to touch. "Get over here, then."

There was more rustling as Scott shuffled closer, and then their bare knees bumped. It had been too hot to get into sleeping bags, so they'd unzipped them and were lying on top, uncovered. Scott's skin was hot where they touched, and when he put a tentative hand on Olly's hip, it burned like a brand on the strip of bare skin above Olly's boxers where his T-shirt had ridden up.

A dangerous surge of heat swept through Olly, and he was even more grateful for the darkness as he was getting hard, just from this conversation and Scott's proximity.

Someone needed to make the first move, but Olly was paralysed. Scott's breath on his face was sweet, like the chocolate they'd eaten earlier. Scott moved closer still, closing the gap between them until it was nothing. Their mouths pressed together.

They kept their lips closed at first. Scott's were dry, a little chapped, and he pressed a few light kisses to Olly's lips while Olly lay frozen. Then Scott parted his lips, and there was warm wetness as he swiped at the seam of Olly's mouth with his tongue. It was weird and tickled a bit, but Olly parted his lips so he could use his tongue too. It was awkward, their noses bumped, and Olly felt like he was breathing in Scott's breath and vice versa. Maybe he should be breathing through his nose? The weirdness of it and his worries about doing it wrong killed his dick's interest in the proceedings a little, but that was no bad thing.

Scott pulled away. "It's hard doing it like this on our sides. Lie on your back." He pushed at Olly's shoulder gently.

Olly obliged, and Scott's dark shape loomed over him as he propped himself up over Olly and dipped his head to kiss him again.

It was so much better like this, able to tilt their heads and get a better angle, their mouths sealed together in a deeper kiss. The slide of their tongues was wet—and a little slimy, as Olly had predicted, but in a weird-good way that sparked uncomfortable heat in Olly's groin again. He could feel the warmth of Scott's body through their clothes and the press of his thigh against his hip. Olly opened his mouth wider and Scott kissed him harder. Scott's hand was still on Olly's shoulder and he clutched him so tightly it was almost painful.

Olly clenched his hands into fists by his side. He wanted to touch, to grab Scott and pull him closer, but he was afraid of making this into something it wasn't supposed to be.

The kiss went on and on until Olly started to forget why that was a bad idea. His body took over and his brain shut off, and it wasn't until he made an embarrassing little sound in the back of his throat that reality came rushing back.

Scott broke the kiss. "Is it okay?" His voice was rough and he was breathing hard.

"Yeah." Olly didn't trust himself to elaborate.

Scott huffed out a soft laugh. "Yeah. It's pretty awesome, actually. Now I can see why people like it."

What did that mean? Did that mean Scott liked this, liked kissing Olly? Was he turned on too?

"I think we need to work out what to do with our hands," Olly suggested, eager for more. "Now we've got the mouth thing sussed."

"Like what?"

"I don't know, exactly. Just… like this, maybe?" He lifted a hand and cupped Scott's cheek. It was smooth and soft, like Olly's own. Ben, in their tutor group, had to shave already, but neither Olly nor Scott did. He slid his hand around to the nape of Scott's neck and tugged him back down.

This time the hesitancy was gone. Olly put his other hand on Scott's back so he could feel the tension as Scott held himself over him. It took a while for Scott to remember to move his hand, but when he did, it felt amazing as it slid into Olly's hair, anchoring him in place as Scott's tongue explored his mouth.

Scott was kissing Olly with such determination, such intensity. He must be into this as much as Olly was. It felt dangerous to hope, but Olly couldn't help himself. Maybe, after this, Scott wouldn't be so interested in kissing girls if he found he liked kissing boys—or Olly specifically—as much as he seemed to.

Olly was achingly hard now; they needed to stop this before he embarrassed himself. He moved a hand to Scott's chest and pushed him away.

"What's wrong?" Scott asked, his voice hoarse.

"Nothing…. I just… I needed a timeout."

"Oh."

Was Olly imagining the disappointment in Scott's voice? Scott rolled off and flopped onto his back beside him again. His breathing was ragged in the silence that surrounded them.

Olly's head whirled with questions. Any lingering doubts he might have had about whether he was gay had fled, chased away by the sensation of Scott's lips and the weight of his body. But was it possible that Scott liked him too, the way he liked Scott? The way Scott has kissed him… it felt like he had been into it too.

It had been so hard for Olly to keep his feelings to himself since he'd worked out what he felt for Scott was a lot more complicated than friendship.

The secret he'd been keeping for so long was gnawing at him, tearing its way out, and he couldn't keep it to himself anymore.

"Scott, I'm gay."

The words burst out, louder than he'd intended, and almost as soon as they were spoken, he wished he could take them back. But it was too late for that.

His declaration was met with a long silence. Olly's thudding heart measured out the time as he waited for Scott to say something.

"Um. Okay."

"Okay what? What does that mean?" Olly didn't know what he'd been expecting, but he needed more than that.

"I don't know. Thanks for telling me, I guess? I don't know what else to say." Scott's voice was weird, tight and uncomfortable, the way he sounded when he was talking to a stranger and feeling awkward. "But I'm not… you know, *gay*." The word came out sounding like something dirty. "I like girls."

Olly's gut twisted unpleasantly. It wasn't exactly a surprise to hear Scott's words, but that kiss had felt like it meant something. "But you said you liked kissing me," he said in a small voice, hating how miserable he sounded.

"Well, yeah. I mean… it was okay. But I'm into girls, not boys. While we were doing it, I was imagining you were Jennifer. I think that's why I liked it."

And just like that, all Olly's hopes were dashed. Smashed to pieces with a few words. Of course Scott had been thinking about a girl while Olly nearly came in his pants from kissing him. Because Scott wasn't interested in boys, and he never would be. Olly was stupid to have hoped that a few kisses might be enough to make Scott want the same things he did.

Tears stung his eyelids, and he was glad for the darkness that hid his humiliation. He swallowed down on the lump in his throat.

"I'm sorry, Olly," Scott said softly. "And I won't tell anyone. You know… what you just told me."

"Yeah. Whatever." Olly forced the words out. He didn't want to talk about it anymore. "Forget I ever said anything. I want to go to sleep now."

Sleep was the farthest thing from his mind, but he was done with this conversation. Done with letting Scott practice his tonsil hockey skills on him, ready to unleash them on Jennifer.

Olly turned away, pulled his sleeping bag around him, and zipped it closed to form a barrier between them. He listened to the sound of Scott doing the same and then flopping onto his back with a sigh.

Scott's breathing gradually slowed and turned into the rhythm of sleep.

84

Olly lay awake beside him, his heart aching and eyes burning with unshed tears because this was the beginning of the end for their friendship. Tonight had ruined everything.

The sounds of a text arriving on Scott's phone jerked Olly back to the present. He opened his eyes and blinked. Tears had leaked out of the corners of his eyes, and he wiped them away.

The phone chimed again, and then again. Olly got it out of his pocket and scowled the screen.

Amy, of course.

She'd been a pain in the arse all day after Scott had dropped Olly in it this morning. She'd badgered Olly to meet her after school, which he'd done while Scott was at the rehearsal, but she was annoyed when he refused to come out and see her that evening. She was babysitting for one of her neighbour's toddlers and insisted that the kid always slept, so Scott should come over and they could "watch Netflix together." Olly was pretty sure she didn't have any intention of actually watching Netflix, and while he was prepared to try and keep her happy for Scott's sake, he had his limits.

He'd claimed his parents wouldn't let him out because he was supposed to be revising. He didn't think it would go down very well if he mentioned he was seeing "Olly" again—even with the excuse of a fake Biology project.

Are you sure you can't come over? read the first text.
Even just for half an hour? The second.
And finally, *I can think of lots of fun things we could do in half an hour... ;)*

Olly shuddered, then felt guilty. Poor Amy. It wasn't her fault her boyfriend's body had been taken over by a gay boy who found her completely unappealing. Amy was probably awesome if you were into girls.

I'm sorry. I can't.

He set the phone aside and curled up, hugging the pillow. The phone buzzed again, but he ignored it. He didn't have the mental energy to try and suck up to Amy anymore. He was tired, and the whole Scott-Marcus thing had dredged up too many uncomfortable emotions. He needed to try and get himself back on an even keel before facing Scott again later.

Dinner with Scott's parents was a barrel of laughs again—*not*. When he told them he was going over to Olly's house, Scott's father raised a disapproving eyebrow that said as much as his words had done the previous day.

"Make sure you're back here by ten, as it's a school night."

Scott's mum didn't say anything, but she pressed her lips together and a worried frown creased her brow.

Olly's appetite vanished. It was hard to eat when you were sitting at a table with people who obviously thought so little of you.

After the meal, it was a relief to get away from the uncomfortable atmosphere and escape to his own house—even if his family treated him like an outsider.

Sophie answered the door. "You again?" She looked him up and down.

"Yep. 'Fraid so." Olly shrugged and grinned.

"Olly!" she yelled. "It's Scott for you."

Olly still wasn't used to the weirdness of hearing his own voice from a distance. "Send him through to the kitchen, I'm washing up."

Olly found Scott up to his elbows in suds as he washed the dishes. Olly's mum was sitting at the table with a cup of tea.

"Hi, Olly. Hi, Mrs Harper," Olly said. His heart squeezed as his mum looked up and gave him a cautious smile. He could really have used a hug from her this evening.

"Hey. I'm almost finished here." Scott glanced at Olly and gave him a tense smile, which Olly returned.

Olly's anger from earlier had faded, and he felt more sad than anything now. He'd never stopped missing their friendship, and getting to spend all this time with Scott this week was bittersweet. The connection between them was still there, but it only reminded Olly that friendship hadn't been enough for him.

He looked more closely at what Scott was doing and frowned. "You should be wearing gloves."

"What? Why? The water's not that hot."

"Because I... um." He glanced at his mum, remembering just in time. "Won't it dry your skin out?"

Olly's mum gave him a curious look as she chipped in. "Scott's right, darling. You know you get eczema if you don't use gloves. What were you thinking?"

"I forgot. But I'm done now." Scott put the last pan on the rack and dried his hands on a tea towel.

Up in his room, Olly made Scott put some cream on his hands.

"But I hate them feeling greasy," Scott complained.

"You'll hate them being sore and itchy more."

Olly grabbed his hands and massaged the cream into them. From the outside, Olly admired his own slim, strong fingers. He'd never thought of himself as having nice hands before, but they were attractive. Scott's were nice too, larger and rougher than Olly's, with a sprinkling of blond hairs on the back of them.

When Olly glanced up from their joined hands, Scott was staring at him; there was a flush on his cheeks that sparked matching heat in Olly's.

He dropped Scott's hands quickly and cleared his throat. "I'm sorry I yelled at you earlier… about the Marcus thing. I get that you were just trying not to blow your cover."

Scott's cheeks turned pink. He looked down at his hands, now twisted in his lap. "That's okay. I'm sorry if I've made things awkward for you."

"You can sort it out with him tomorrow. But be gentle with him, yeah? He's a nice guy."

"Will do."

"Oh, that reminds me," Olly said. "You should probably text Amy. She keeps texting, and I'm running out of things to say to her."

Olly had found four more texts from Amy before he'd gone down to dinner, and the last one was bitching about him not replying. He handed the phone to Scott and let him read through the message history.

"I'm sorry I dropped you… I mean me… or us, whatever, in it this morning." Scott sighed. "I should have checked what you'd already told her."

"Yeah. She wasn't happy."

"God, it's so hard dealing with this stuff when we're like this. It's bad enough normally, but now it's impossible. Maybe I should just break up with her. This whole situation isn't fair on her anyway. It's pretty creepy, when you think about it."

"But it's not going to last forever." As he said it, Olly realised they had no way of knowing for sure. But no, they had to trust this was temporary. The thought of spending the rest of his life in someone else's body was terrifying. "Dumping your girlfriend seems a bit drastic. I'm sure we can make it work."

"I'd been thinking about finishing with her anyway, even before all this happened."

Olly didn't like the way his heart leaped at that. It shouldn't matter to him whether Scott was single or not. "Yeah?" he said cautiously.

"Yeah. I mean, we haven't been together long, and it was never serious."

Olly raised his eyebrows. "You sure about that?"

Scott huffed in exasperation. "Well, it wasn't serious for me. That's why I was thinking about breaking up with her. She seems way keener than I am, so it seemed unfair to string her along."

"Have you ever had a girlfriend for more than a few weeks?"

Scott glared. "Have you ever had a boyfriend for more than a few weeks?"

Touché.

Olly turned the conversation back to the matter in hand. "So, do you really want to break up with her?"

"Yeah."

"Do you want me to do it for you?"

Scott shrugged. "I suppose. I don't want to do it by text, because I don't want to be *that* guy."

"So instead you're going to get your friend to do it." Olly chuckled. "I'm not sure that's much better, Scott."

Scott grinned sheepishly. "Yeah, well. It's my best option right now."

They smiled at each other for a moment, and it was only then that Olly realised he'd just referred to himself as Scott's friend. He hadn't thought of them in that way for years. Scott's easy acceptance of it made something warm blossom in Olly's chest.

"Okay, so… should I phone her?"

"No, not while she's babysitting. Talk to her face-to-face at school tomorrow."

"And what should I tell her? It's not you, it's me?" Olly snorted. "Which is so ridiculously true, she has no idea."

"Just tell her I really like her but I want to focus on my exams and we're going to be going our separate ways at the end of summer anyway, so I don't want to get into anything serious right now."

"Oh, good. That should work." Olly nodded. "Where are you going next year, by the way?"

"Manchester, if I get the grades."

"Seriously?" A smile crept over Olly's face.

"Yeah, why?"

"Because that's my first choice too." Olly watched Scott carefully for his reaction and was rewarded when Scott's face lit up.

Scott said, "That's cool. Maybe we can… hang out or something?"

"Yeah. I'd like that."

There was a long pause.

"Does this mean we're friends again?" Scott asked, sounding hopeful.

"Yeah, I guess we are." Olly wanted that. But he couldn't help wanting more. Eager to change the subject, he picked up the script for the play. "So, we'd better get started on this. You have a ton of lines to learn for the next rehearsal on Friday. It's the scene at the party where they meet for the first time, and you have a lot to say."

Olly sat on his bed; Scott flopped down beside him and leaned close so he could see the page. They started to read through the lines together, repeating them over and over until Scott could remember them. When they got to the part where Romeo and Juliet have to kiss, Scott asked, "What sort of kiss is it? Like a peck on the lips or what?"

"The first one's a peck, the second one's more of a snog. But we can go through that tomorrow with all the movements and blocking."

"Okay." Scott swallowed hard.

Olly's heart thumped a little faster. Would Scott actually want to kiss him, or would he just want Olly to explain what he had to do?

By the time they were done, they were both yawning.

"My head feels like it's going to explode with all the words I've crammed into it." Scott rubbed his temples.

"Yeah. You've done well. If we go through it again tomorrow, it should be enough to save my arse from the wrath of Miss Andrews." Olly glanced sidelong at Scott and added softly, "Thanks so much for doing this."

"I don't have much choice in the matter." Scott shrugged, but he smiled too, and looked almost flirtatious as he gazed back from under the dark lashes that fringed his green eyes.

Olly knew his eyes were one of his best features, and he'd used them to his advantage in the past. It was weird having his secret weapon turned on him. He wondered whether Scott had any idea he was doing it.

Olly got up and stretched until his back cracked. "I'd better head back to your place. It's nearly ten, and I don't want to piss your parents off."

Scott saw Olly to the front door. "See you tomorrow."

"Yeah, I'll call for you at the usual time."

"Night."

"Goodnight."

They exchanged a brief smile before Olly turned away and heard the door close softly behind him.

CHAPTER EIGHT

Later that night, Scott lay wide awake long after the rest of the house was asleep. Restless and confused, he couldn't get comfortable in Olly's bed, no matter how many times he changed position. His head was full of kissing Marcus and how it had felt—including how freeing it had been to be able to kiss another boy without worrying what anyone would think.

As he remembered the sensation of Marcus's lips and hands, his body reacted, flooding with arousal. But then the memory of Marcus faded, overlaid by Olly and that night in the tent when they were fourteen. Scott had kissed a lot of girls since then, and he'd never experienced a fraction of the thrill he'd felt during his first kiss with his then best friend. Kissing Olly had been the best and the worst thing that had ever happened to him. It had made him question things he wasn't ready to question, and it had cost him his friendship with Olly—even though Scott didn't fully understand why.

Scott groaned, trying to ignore the insistent press of his cock in the stupid tight briefs Olly wore.

There was no way he'd be able to get to sleep unless he got himself off. Olly wouldn't care, surely? He'd probably think it was funny that Scott was touching his dick. Scott slid a hand down to squeeze the erection in his underwear and gasped at the touch. This wasn't going to take long, and it was a biological necessity—like going to the toilet. He needed it; Olly's body needed it. If he thought about it like that, then he was doing Olly a favour.

His skin prickled with sweat as he started to rub himself through the fabric, so he pushed the duvet down and took off his T-shirt. He ran his free hand over the smooth skin of his chest—Olly's chest. It felt different to his own, sensitive in subtly different places. When he touched them, Olly's nipples didn't react as much as his own did, but as he slid his hand lower to toy with the faint line of hair below his belly button, he shivered. It felt so good.

A wet patch formed where the head of his cock pressed tight against the material. Scott finally gave in to the temptation to push the waistband down and give himself the skin-on-skin contact he craved.

He let out a gasp, curving his hips up into the touch and thrusting into the grip of his fist.

I'm touching Olly's cock. This is so fucking weird.

He looked down, but with the blinds shut, he could barely make out anything other than the faintest movement as he stroked himself. Without thinking too much about what he was doing and why, Scott stopped long enough to turn the lamp by the bed back on.

The sight of pale limbs, dark pubes, and the flushed head of Olly's cock poking out of his fist with every stroke nearly sent Scott into orbit. He stroked harder, faster, and in a matter of minutes, he came all over himself with a muffled groan.

As soon as the waves of pleasure receded, guilt crept in to take its place. His cheeks burned with shame, but the memory of how good it had been only raised more questions. Scott couldn't deny that part of what made it so hot was because it was Olly's body he was touching, Olly's dick he'd been stroking rather than his own.

Heart still thudding hard, Scott stared at the ceiling as the come cooled on his stomach and his thoughts whirled, his mind taking him back to that night in the tent again and how he'd felt when they kissed.

It had been more than friends experimenting, so much more. But Scott had buried his attraction. He'd lied to Olly and hidden it even from himself—because he was afraid. He wanted to like girls, to take the easy option, and didn't want to have to deal with the fallout. Not so much from his friends, but from his family, especially his father. So he'd dated girls, kissed girls, tried to find a girl who made him feel even a tiny hint of what he'd experienced with Olly.

But none of them came close.

It had always been Olly.

The next morning, Scott was still in Olly's body when he woke. Rekindling their friendship obviously wasn't the magic solution to get them back to normal, but at least it made spending time together easier.

Olly called for Scott again and was revving the engine as he hurried down the path.

"All right, all right. I'm coming." Scott slammed the door and strapped himself in as Olly pulled away.

"How are you?" Olly asked.

"Tired."

Scott couldn't look him in the eye. His head was still full of what he'd done last night. It seemed wrong, somehow, doing that without permission. Maybe he should have asked Olly first, but how fucking awkward would that conversation be?

"Yeah." Olly sounded as tense as Scott felt.

Scott studied him more carefully—he looked tired too. As he watched, Olly shifted in his seat.

"Are you okay?" Scott asked.

Olly glanced sideways and caught Scott looking. He grimaced, turning his attention back to the road. "Just horny. You know how it is. Your morning wood is very persistent today." He reached down to adjust himself. "I assume you're having similar issues now it's been a couple of days."

Scott's cheeks flamed as he desperately tried to think of an answer that wouldn't give him away. "Um… yeah," he managed in a choked voice.

Olly snapped his head around again and narrowly missed clipping a parked car.

Scott yelled, "Eyes on the road! Jesus."

The car slowed, and Olly parked at the side of the street. He turned and fixed his gaze on Scott. "You had a wank." He narrowed his eyes, and his voice was half-accusing, half-amused.

Scott wanted the passenger seat to swallow him, but he tried to brazen it out. "I had to! I couldn't sleep."

"Nor could I. But I thought it would be weird jerking off when it's not my dick."

"It *was* weird, but I needed to, okay?" He didn't add that as well as being weird it had also been disturbingly hot.

Olly's expression morphed into a smug smile. "I can't believe that you cracked first! That will teach me to try and be all honourable about it. I didn't think you'd want me touching your dick... not like that, anyway. But now I assume you're okay with it?"

"Yeah, sure," Scott said gruffly.

He could hardly refuse. He tried to banish intrusive images of Olly touching his dick when they were back in their own bodies.

"Just so we're clear," Olly said, "where do you stand on arseplay?"

Scott's eyes flew wide, but before he could answer, Olly burst out laughing.

"Oh my God, your face! It's okay, I was kidding. I mean... not that I'm averse to that myself. But don't worry, Scott, I won't go there with yours."

Scott glared at him. His cheeks felt as though they were about to burst into flames at any minute. He was such a confusing mixture of embarrassed, turned on, and freaked out. "Just drive," he finally said.

Once the car was moving again and Scott's arousal and blushes had faded, Olly asked, "So, are you sure you want me to break up with Amy today? She keeps texting you again this morning. I did reply to try and keep her happy, but I didn't say much. Just 'good morning' and 'see you at school.'"

Scott hadn't given any thought to Amy this morning. His head had been too full of Olly. He supposed that only made the decision easier. Amy deserved better than a boyfriend who was obsessed with someone else. "Yeah," he said with a sigh. "Get it over with."

"I thought I'd talk to her at the start of lunch," Olly said. "That way, she's got her friends around."

"Sounds good." Not that there was ever a good time to dump someone, but there was no point in dragging it out when Scott was sure it was the right decision.

They went their separate ways when they got to school. Scott found Marcus hanging around near Olly's locker, clearly waiting for him.

"Hi, Olly." He gave Scott a shy, flirtatious smile. "I was wondering if you wanted to get together after school today?"

It looked like Olly wouldn't be the only one disappointing people today.

"Yeah, I'm sorry, but no."

"Oh." Marcus's face fell. "After yesterday I thought maybe you'd want to hang out."

"Yesterday was—" 'A mistake' sounded too harsh, so he tried to find better words. "—it was good, but I'm not interested in taking it any further."

Marcus lowered his voice. "Is it because of Scott?"

"What?" Scott said in surprise. "No. Why would it be anything to do with him?"

"Just the way he looked at us when he caught us kissing. He was really pissed off. I thought maybe he was jealous, and that you and him were involved somehow. I know he's not out, but…."

Scott felt a lurch of anxiety. What if Marcus had shared his theory with anyone else? Gossip travelled at lightning speed in school. "No. It's not like that. Scott's straight. We're just friends."

Even as he said it, he knew it for the lie it was. He wasn't straight. He never had been, and he never would be, no matter how much he tried to convince himself.

"Okay, okay, whatever. It's not my business anyway." Marcus backed away, lifting his hands in a defensive gesture.

It was only then that Scott realised he'd clenched his fists and was frowning. He forced himself to relax. "Anyway, yeah. I'm sorry again, but I'd rather be friends."

"No worries." Marcus looked relieved that the conversation was over. He turned and went, leaving Scott standing by Olly's locker, wondering whether his life could get any more complicated. He really hoped not.

At lunchtime, Scott was on edge, looking out for Olly and Amy and wondering whether Olly had spoken to her yet, but he didn't catch sight of either of them in the cafeteria.

"Have you got your lines learned for the scene tomorrow?" Demi asked. "Do you want to run through them with me?"

"Yeah, just about." Scott had spent hours on them last night, but it wouldn't hurt to go through them again.

It was sunny outside, so he and Demi sat in a shady spot at the edge of the playing fields and read through the scene a few times. Scott was relieved to find that he remembered the lines well. Sleeping on them seemed to have helped. Thank goodness he was a fast learner, but his exam revision was inevitably suffering. There was only so much space in his head for new information.

He got a text from Olly just before the end of lunch.

The deed is done. You're single again.
How did she take it?
There were tears and some shouting, and then more tears. I think she's gone home sick for the afternoon.

Scott's stomach twisted as guilt shot through him. Poor Amy.

I hope you let her down as gently as you could.
I did my best.
Scott sighed. *Thanks.*

On the way home, Scott said. "Let's go to my house." He hadn't set foot in there since the morning they'd woken up changed. He wanted to see his room and spend some time there.

"Are you sure?" Something in Olly's tone made Scott jerk his head up and study his profile. There was a tightness to his jaw, and he was frowning.

"Yeah. Why? Every time I suggest it, you find an excuse to go to yours instead."

Olly swallowed and gripped the wheel a little tighter. "Well…. I don't think your parents like me very much. They've been a bit weird about me going over to yours the last two nights. So I wasn't sure if it's such a good idea for you to be there."

A cold chill crept through Scott as he imagined what Olly might have heard from his parents. "What have they said?"

"Just that you shouldn't spend too much time with *boys like that*," Olly's tone was bitter; the hurt seeped through and made Scott's stomach tighten with anger. "Those were your dad's exact words."

"Fuck, Olly. I'm so sorry."

Olly shrugged but didn't reply.

"Let's go to your house again, then," Scott said. Suddenly his home was much less appealing, and the thought that Olly had to go back there and listen to his father spouting shit like that made him feel sick.

Once they were settled in Olly's room with mugs of tea and a packet of chocolate biscuits, Scott brought the subject up again.

"I'm really sorry about my dad." He felt guilty by association.

"I didn't know your dad was homophobic."

"Why would you? He doesn't put up banners or anything. But yeah, he is. He made a right fuss about it when gay marriage was made legal. 'Why do they care about getting married anyway? They're all promiscuous anyway... blah-blah-blah.'" Scott's anger rose at the memory. He'd tried to argue with his dad about it and even involve his mum. But she refused to be drawn in, and his dad wouldn't budge on his viewpoint.

"Wanker!" Olly exclaimed. "Sorry, Scott. I know he's your dad, but what does he fucking know? That's such a generalisation."

"Tell me about it." Scott sighed. "The thing is, with him... it's personal."

He lowered his voice, even though they were in Olly's room with the door closed. His dad would go mental if he found out Scott had shared their deepest, darkest family secret. "His dad was gay, and he cheated on his mum for years with random blokes. But then he got caught with some man in a park and arrested by the police for gross indecency. When it all came out, my gran was devastated. She left him, took my dad and my auntie with her. Dad was about fourteen at the time and he hasn't seen his dad since. He doesn't even know I know. My mum told me because I asked why we didn't have any photos of granddad. They told me he died, but I don't know if that's true." Scott trailed off, realising he was rambling.

Olly was silent for a minute, frowning as he digested the information. "That sucks... for your gran and your dad, I mean. But it doesn't give him the right to assume that all gay men are like that."

"I know." Scott agreed totally. He wasn't going to argue. He'd grown up listening to his dad make homophobic comments about celebrities or commenting negatively on LGBT-related news stories. He was tired of hearing it.

"I feel kind of sad for your grandfather too, though." Olly bit his lip, glancing sideways at Scott. "Not that he didn't do anything wrong... but it must have been hard for him. Keeping that secret all those years, being too afraid to come out, cheating on his wife with random blokes, and never having the chance to fall in love."

Scott suddenly found he had a lump in his throat. His own secret was threatening to burst out of him, but now wasn't the right time. Maybe once things were back to normal, he could talk to Olly about the stuff he was finally admitting to himself. He swallowed hard. "Yeah." He cleared his throat. "Okay, we'd better get on with this scene. I can't come back after dinner because I need to spend some time revising. I'm really behind, with everything that's happened this week."

"If we're still stuck in the wrong bodies once the exams start, we're fucked, no matter how much revision we do," Olly said gloomily.

It was a chilling thought. If Scott didn't get the grades for uni, he'd probably be stuck at home while he retook his A levels, and his dad would make his life a misery. Unfortunately the only subject they shared was Biology. Even though both of them were good students, there was no way they could cram two years' worth of work in a few weeks.

Scott tried to sound confident. "We'll work it out by then. There must be a way we can fix this. We'll find out how. But for now we just have to make the best of it without messing up each other's lives, and this afternoon that means focusing on getting me up to scratch for your bloody rehearsal tomorrow."

"Okay." Olly gave him a small smile. "Let's do it."

They read through the scene first to check Scott knew the lines. He was almost word perfect.

"Romeo's so fickle," Scott said. "He goes from being totally in love with that other bird to head-over-heels for Juliet as soon as he sees her."

"It's not love, though, is it?" Olly shrugged. "It's lust. He's being led by his dick rather than his emotions."

"I suppose." Scott wasn't sure he was qualified to judge. He'd never had that experience: a bolt of love or lust totally out of the blue that made a person do stupid, ridiculous things. Not the way it was in books or movies. "Have you ever felt like that about anyone?"

"No," Olly said shortly. "I mean… I've looked at people and thought they're hot, but I never thought I was in love with any of them. I don't believe in love at first sight. I think love is something that grows out of knowing someone, out of being friends with them as much as wanting to shag them."

Scott was silent, but his heart did a hopeful flip at Olly's words. Was there any chance Olly could have felt like that about him once? Could he still feel that way, or was it too late? An idea took hold, forming in his brain and finding its way out of his mouth before he could think better of it.

"Let's run through the scene again, but I want to act it out this time. Can you show me what I need to do, so I know for tomorrow?"

Olly's gaze flicked up to meet Scott's and he ran a nervous hand through his hair. "Okay. Well, there isn't a lot of movement." He got up and stood in the space between his bed and the desk. His room was small, so there wasn't a lot of room to manoeuvre. "Juliet will be standing front stage right, and you enter from the left." He gestured for Scott to stand too. "When you approach her, she doesn't see you at first, and you ask the servant about her and make your first speech about how hot she is. Then there's the bit with Tybalt and Capulet. During that time, just keep staring at Juliet. But then, once they're finished with their lines, Juliet turns and you stare at each other. You need to look totally goofy and love-struck."

It was hard trying to look love-struck by staring at his own face, but when Scott reminded himself it was Olly on the inside, it suddenly got much easier.

"Yeah, that's good," Olly said. "And Demi will look back at you the same way."

Their gazes locked and held, and it was the weirdest sensation. Even though Scott was staring into his own blue eyes instead of Olly's green ones, he felt as if he could see Olly anyway, like he was staring into his soul and the outer shell didn't matter anymore.

"Now you talk to her." Olly's voice was a little hoarse. "And gradually move closer, until you take her hands during the last two lines before the kiss."

Scott started speaking the lines.

They'd lost all meaning as he'd crammed the information into his reluctant brain over the last twenty-four hours, but saying them now to Olly, the beauty of the language and the weird tension between them lent life to the words. When he took Olly's hands, his heart beat faster.

Olly licked his lips as Scott said, "Thus from my lips by thine, my sin is purg'd...."

He closed the gap between them. Because of the height difference, he had to tilt his face up a little to meet Olly's, and the weirdness that he was basically kissing himself came rushing back in, making him clumsy. He pulled away quickly when he remembered it was only supposed to be a peck on the lips.

Olly's pupils were huge and his cheeks flushed as he brought a hand up and touched his mouth with his fingertips for a moment. He sounded awed as he spoke the next line. "Then have my lips the sin that they have took?"

Acting on instinct rather than instruction, Scott took Olly's face in both hands and held his gaze. "Sin from my lips, oh trespass sweetly urg'd. Give me my sin again!" And he kissed him for the second time. Longer, sweeter, their lips parting softly.

Scott found himself wishing this was real, wishing it meant something, wishing with all his heart that he was in his own body with Olly kissing him back. The kiss stretched out, expanding in his consciousness, but in reality it was only a few seconds before he reluctantly drew away again.

"You kiss by the book," Olly said huskily, lips still parted.

They stared at each other. Scott's heart was an insistent pulse, a drumbeat drowning out coherent thought. He wanted to kiss Olly again—a real kiss, not a kiss because they were rehearsing a play. He clenched his fists to stop himself reaching out and pulling Olly into his arms.

Olly cleared his throat, breaking the spell. "So, yeah... that was, uh. Yeah. Perfect. And then the nurse comes along and cockblocks them."

Scott chuckled ironically, thinking he knew exactly how his character must feel. "Yeah. Poor old Romeo."

"And after that you get a bit of a break until the balcony scene. Shall we run through that one next?"

"Sure." Scott's pulse had settled now. He pushed away all thoughts of kissing Olly again. It was madness. He was as bad as Romeo, suddenly wanting to declare his feelings for Olly after four years of them barely being civil to each other. "Let's sit down again to read it through. I think I know most of the words."

By the time they'd finished, Scott was as prepared as he'd ever be for the rehearsal tomorrow.

"Good luck with the revision," Olly said as Scott saw him out.

"Yeah, you too."

"And I'll pick you up tomorrow morning like normal?"

"Sure." Scott sighed.

When had being stuck in Olly's body and not being able to drive his own car become his new normal? They needed to find the key to get themselves back where they should be—in their own bodies, living their own lives. If rekindling their friendship was the answer, surely they must be nearly there by now?

Maybe the kiss would do it?

Scott snorted at the fanciful idea, feeling foolish. But when he thought about it, it might not be such a crazy idea after all. Perhaps they'd wake up tomorrow morning and everything would be back to normal.

He could only hope.

CHAPTER NINE

Olly spent another joyless evening at Scott's house. Dinner was the usual tense occasion. Luckily, Scott's dad was stressed about some issue at work and most of the parental conversation focused on that. Olly got away with eating in silence and escaped to Scott's room as soon as he'd helped clear away.

He managed to finish a Psychology essay—his last for the year. He'd emailed it to himself from his own laptop earlier so he could work on it here. Then he sent it back to his computer, with instructions for Scott to email it to Olly's teacher.

After that was done, he lay on Scott's bed with his English Lit notes and tried to revise, but his mind wouldn't settle on the words. Flitting butterfly-like, he kept jumping from worry to worry.

How was he going to get through football training again without fucking up? According to Scott's phone calendar, a match was scheduled for Monday, and that would be even more stressful. Then the play… and not to mention their A levels looming on the horizon made it the most important couple of months of their lives so far, and this situation threatened to ruin everything.

Could the kiss make a difference?

Olly's heart beat faster as he remembered the weird sensation of kissing Scott—but not Scott—earlier. They'd only been acting, but it inevitably made him think about their other kiss. The one that *had* been real, for Olly at least.

He frowned at the page in front of him; he'd been doodling as his mind wandered. Leaves and flowers covered the page, twisting and tangled like the thoughts in his head.

Was it possible that something as simple as a kiss could reverse whatever had happened to make them this way? If this was a fairy story or a Hollywood movie—and it certainly felt like he was living in one—then a kiss should break the spell. Hope swelled in his chest, fizzing through his veins and lifting his spirits. Maybe this was it, they'd wake up tomorrow, and everything would be back to normal. No more football training, no more godawful Business Studies and Economics lessons, no more dealing with Scott's dad being a twat.

Later that night, when he was in bed, Olly let himself remember the kiss again. He brought a hand up and traced the shape of his lips with a fingertip, imagining how it would feel to be back in his own body, kissing Scott for real. The memory of the kiss in the tent merged with his fantasies, and he closed his eyes, letting arousal take hold. In his imagination they were themselves again, kissing passionately, with no hesitation or uncertainty. He ran his fingers over the stubble on his jaw, imagining Scott doing the same. After rolling onto his side, Olly buried his face in the pillow and inhaled the scent of Scott; his parted lips brushed against the cotton, and he gasped.

Fuck it. Scott did it first.

Olly reached down, pushed a hand into Scott's baggy boxers, and curled his fingers around his erection. The touch he was so desperate for made him moan. He bit his lips, trying to stay quiet in the night-time silence.

It didn't take long. A few days of building tension and the scent of Scott soon had Olly fucking his fist as the pillow stifled his ragged breathing. When he came, it was fierce, his body tense and shaking with the force of it. He caught the come in his hand, and before he had time to think about what he was doing, he licked his fingers clean, imagining he was sucking Scott's dick. The thought sent another pulse of pleasure rippling through him.

He turned onto his back and stared into the darkness. As the high of his orgasm receded, despondency rushed back in to fill the space. He was in the wrong body, living the wrong life. Trapped in a situation he couldn't control, all his carefully buried feelings for Scott were coming back to haunt him.

Fuck his life, seriously. Fuck it so hard.

The next morning, Olly overslept because he'd forgotten to set Scott's alarm clock, but a text chime from Scott's phone woke him. He sighed heavily as he realised he was still in Scott's bed and Scott's body. Exhausted and irritable, he'd lain awake for too long last night, lost in a downward spiral of negative thoughts.

The text was from Scott.

Don't forget to pack football kit.

Olly threw on the same clothes he'd worn yesterday, forgoing a shower. Breakfast was a slice of bread and jam, eaten while putting on his shoes and packing the stuff he needed for the day. Scott's dad was long gone, thankfully, and his mum was getting ready for work, so their paths barely crossed.

When he screeched to a halt outside his house, Scott was waiting on the doorstep with his eyebrows raised and arms folded.

"Cutting it a bit fine this morning, aren't you?"

"I couldn't sleep," Olly replied shortly.

"Got my football kit?"

"Yes. Got your script for rehearsal after school? And can you remember what you need to do?"

"Yes, and yes," said Scott. "But I was thinking maybe we could get together at lunchtime to go over some team tactics and set plays—just to get you up to speed for football practice later?"

"Yeah, that's probably a good idea. I had trouble connecting with some of the passes last time."

The rest of the way to school, they didn't talk. Olly was unhappily wrapped in his own thoughts, and Scott was equally pensive.

As soon as they arrived at school, it was clear that something was going on.

The first clue was a group of girls from their year, who were hanging around in the hallway as they entered. The girls stared blatantly as Olly and Scott walked past, and then one of them whispered something behind her hand and the others giggled.

"What the hell was that about?" Olly asked once they were out of earshot.

"No clue." Scott shrugged.

Everything was fine for the rest of the morning. Olly made it through double Economics without falling asleep. He had one dicey moment when the teacher called on him to answer a question, but he faked confusion until she rolled her eyes and directed the question to another student instead.

At break time he couldn't face hanging out with Scott's mates, so he hid in the library and skimmed a chapter in a Psych book on hallucinations. He couldn't help wondering if that was what this was. Maybe he was crazy, or maybe he'd been in an accident and was in a coma and this whole thing was just a weird dream. He pinched himself again to check. It still hurt, but he wasn't sure that proved anything.

In their Biology lesson before lunch, things took another turn for the weird.

As Olly came into the room, Amy's friend Isobel gave him a look that made his balls shrivel. Seriously. If looks could kill, he was dead—probably having died in a slow and painful fashion involving genital torture. He set his jaw and glared back. For fuck's sake, it wasn't like Amy and Scott's relationship had been serious. People broke up. Shit happened.

Isobel smirked and said something in an undertone to the girl sitting beside her.

The other girl's eyes flew open in surprise and she turned really obviously in her seat to stare at Scott at the back of the room. She swivelled her head to look at Olly, and then back at Scott again before turning back to Amy, a combination of disbelief and glee on her face.

"No way?" Her shocked whisper carried across the room.

"Apparently." Isobel shrugged.

Olly's cheeks burned; a cold lump of dread settled in his stomach.

What the fuck is going on?

He flashed a look at Scott, but Scott had his head down and was doodling in the margin of his notebook, seemingly oblivious to any drama.

Ignoring the girls, Olly took Scott's usual seat next to Marty. "Alright?" Olly muttered.

"Hiya." Marty looked troubled, his usually amiable features marred by a frown. "You okay?"

"Yeah, just tired." That much was true, at least. His late night was blurring his brain and feeding the irritation that simmered under his skin.

At the end of Biology, Olly was packing up his books when Scott approached him.

"Hey," Scott said.

"Hi." Olly zipped up his bag.

Marty looked at Scott, and a frown furrowed his brow again. To Olly, he said, "You ready, man? It's fish and chips day today, and I'm starving."

"Uh—" Olly looked at Scott. "—I have to talk to Olly about, um, stuff. So I'm just gonna grab something from the sandwich bar."

He winced at how weird he sounded. For fuck's sake, he'd make a terrible spy. It was a good thing his country was never likely to depend on him for matters of national security.

"Oh, okay." Marty shouldered his bag and shot Scott a suspicious look. "Well, I'll see you later, then."

He went, leaving them alone, the last two in the classroom.

"Ugh, sorry." Olly grimaced. "That wasn't exactly smooth. I'm not quite with it today."

"Are you all right?"

"I'm just tired. This whole thing is messing with my head, and I didn't sleep well."

They went to the cafeteria and bought sandwiches and cans of Coke to take outside. Maybe Olly was being paranoid, but he couldn't shake the feeling that people were looking at them strangely. He caught Amy's eye and gave her an apologetic half-smile, expecting her to blank him but feeling like he owed it to her to be civil.

She smirked back, oddly smug for someone who professed to be heartbroken yesterday. He was glad when he and Scott reached the front of the queue and could pay and get the hell out of there.

They sat under a tree at the edge of the playing fields and leaned against the trunk with their shoulders brushing as they ate their lunch.

Scott went over some team signals and tactics they'd been working on, sketching out diagrams for Olly on a notepad. Olly studied them and asked a few questions here and there.

"Okay," he finally said. "I'll do my best not to fuck up tonight."

"And Monday," Scott said gloomily. "There's a match on Monday."

"Yeah." Olly's stomach lurched with nerves at the thought of it. "I keep hoping this might be over by then."

"Me too." Scott was pulling the petals off a daisy one by one. His voice was tight. "I thought us kissing might do it. Is that crazy?" He huffed out a laugh. "Like the Frog Prince or Sleeping Beauty or something. Jesus, what an idiot."

Olly turned to look at him. He wondered if he'd ever get used to seeing his own face from the outside. It was so weird thinking that Scott's... what? His *soul* was in there, Scott's thoughts and feelings hiding behind Olly's sharp features and cool green eyes. "I wondered too, so I don't think it's crazy at all. But I guess it wasn't the answer."

Scott's gaze dropped and Olly licked his lips nervously. A tingle of something rippled through him and he realised he was getting hard.

What the fuck? No.

He drew his knees up to hide it and looked away quickly. Other students were starting to drift back across the playing fields towards the school buildings. Lunch must be nearly over. "We should probably get back."

"Yeah." Scott stood first and hesitated a moment before holding out a hand to Olly, who took it.

Scott hauled him up. "Jesus, I didn't realise how heavy I was," he puffed. "Or maybe you're just a weakling."

"Fuck you." Olly shoved Scott, using Scott's superior strength against him to knock him back down. Maybe Scott had a point. It was embarrassingly easy to push his body back down to the ground and pin Scott. He got hold of Scott's wrists and held them over his head, squeezing his thighs around Scott's hips so he couldn't move.

Scott was laughing and protesting, but then he shifted his hips and—

Oh. Olly's semi that hadn't quite gone away from before rubbed against an unmistakable answering hardness.

They froze, staring at each other in shocked surprise.

Thick tension surrounded them, blocking out the rest of the world until a loud wolf whistle made Olly snap his head around. A group of people were watching them. There were several blokes from Scott's team, including Marty, with Hazel and Liam—another guy from the football team who had his arm around Amy.

Wow, she didn't waste any time.

"Hey, homos, get a room!" Liam yelled, grinning.

Some of the group laughed, but Marty and Hazel looked uncomfortable.

"Come on, guys, we're gonna be late," Marty said.

Scott was rigid with tension underneath Olly.

Trying to appear casual and unconcerned, which was a challenge when his heart was beating so hard he thought he might pass out, Olly disentangled himself from Scott and got up slowly. He flipped his middle finger up at Liam.

"Yeah, yeah. Fuck you, arsehole." He really hoped his semi wasn't obvious.

"I'm not into that," Liam retorted. "Didn't know you were either. Or maybe your boyfriend is the one who takes it?"

A wave of red-hot fury surged through Olly and he clenched his fists, turning to square up to Liam. He realised with a thrill that he was taller than Liam, and broader. With Scott's strength and reflexes, he reckoned he could take him. Olly had spent most of his school life avoiding conflict because it usually ended badly for him. But in this body, he felt invincible.

"No!" Scott had got to his feet and grabbed Olly's arm, fingers digging in to the point of pain. "He's just being a twat. It's not worth it. If it comes to a fight, you'll both be in the shit. You could be excluded from school and maybe even kicked off the team."

The urgency in his tone cut through, soothing Olly like cool water on a burn.

"He's right." Marty moved to put himself between them, his hands spread out. "And you've got to play together after school. Calm the fuck down, both of you. Liam, you were well out of order."

There was silence for a moment, and Olly forced himself to breathe, his pulse beating in his ears as his rage subsided slowly. They were right; Liam wasn't worth fucking up Scott's life for. He was just a mouthy homophobe, and sadly there were still too many of them around.

The school bell rang, signalling afternoon registration and interrupting the tension.

Olly uncurled his fists, feeling the sting where his nails had bitten into his palms. He gave Liam the most disparaging look he could manage, then turned to Marty and clapped him on the shoulder. "Yeah, thanks, mate. You're right. He's not worth it."

And with that he turned away, picked up his bag, and stalked across the grass. Scott fell into step beside him.

"Thanks," Scott said quietly. "Much as I wanted you to break his stupid nose, my parents would have gone ballistic if you had."

"You're welcome." Olly rolled his shoulders, and the last of his anger drained away.

Olly was dreading football training even more after the altercation at lunchtime. He kept his head down during his afternoon classes, pretending to be busy taking notes, and avoided Marty's curious gaze. He had a free period last lesson and hid out in the library, trying and failing to work on an Economics assignment while he psyched himself up to face Liam again.

When it was time for practice, he paused at the door of the locker rooms and squared his shoulders, summoning up the courage to stalk in there as though he belonged.

Some of the team were already changing, but a quick glance told him Liam wasn't there yet. Maybe Olly was paranoid, but he felt as if everyone was watching him, sidelong glances that flitted away when he tried to meet their gazes. Probably everyone had heard about the almost-fight at lunchtime.

Marty turned up just after Olly had pulled his shorts on. He arrived with Liam, who seemed to have lost his usual swagger.

"Alright." Marty took the spot beside Olly and started getting changed.

Liam moved into the space on the other side of Olly. But he hesitated, bag in hand and a shamefaced expression on his features. "I'm sorry I was a dick earlier."

Olly hid his surprise. He hadn't seen that apology coming. "Yeah?"

"Yeah. Like... Marty was right. I was out of line, and I shouldn't have said what I did. It's none of my business anyway."

"Um, okay." Olly felt like he'd missed a crucial plot twist.

What was none of Liam's business?

But he didn't have time to ask, because Mr Buckley arrived then and started yelling at them to hurry up and get their lazy arses out on the pitch.

Practice went pretty well, considering. Maybe the residual adrenaline from lunchtime fuelled him, or maybe Scott's extra coaching had worked, but Olly was literally way more on the ball than he'd been at the previous session.

As his nerves settled, he started to enjoy himself, and the icing on the cake was a spectacular goal that he chipped into the top corner of the net after a flawless pass from Liam.

Liam hugged him, all hot-and-sweaty bro bonding, and when he gasped breathlessly in Olly's ear, "Fucking sweet goal, man. That was awesome," Olly felt as though he'd won the lottery.

Afterwards in the locker room, Liam seemed to think he was Olly's—or Scott's—best mate. He showered beside him; clearly not worried about any of the stuff he'd accused Scott of earlier, and nattered away about tactics for Monday and how he reckoned the game was in the bag. After the practice they'd just had, Olly could almost believe him.

Once they were half-dressed, Liam cleared his throat awkwardly. "So, uh. I was thinking I might ask Amy out."

"Oh. Yeah. You should totally do that." Judging by the way Amy had been hanging on Liam's arm earlier, she'd probably be very happy to be asked out by him.

"Cool. Thanks, man."

Olly looked at him blankly. Had he really just given his 'permission' for Liam to ask his ex out? Wow, the whole bro-code thing was weird. They should make a handbook to explain that shit.

As they filed out of the locker room, clean and dressed and ready to head home, Marty tugged on Olly's sleeve. "Can I have a quick word?"

Something in his expression told Olly it was important. He was supposed to be meeting Scott at the car, but hopefully this wouldn't take long. "Sure."

They hung back until they were the only two left in the corridor and the last echoes of footsteps had disappeared around the corner.

"So. Is it true about you and Olly?" Marty asked. His brow furrowed and there was a pinkness to his cheeks. "Don't get me wrong, man. I'm totally okay with it, and I'm on your side, whatever. I'm just… surprised."

Marty wasn't the only one who was surprised.

"What?" Olly gaped at him. "Liam was just being a twat at lunchtime. You saw us, we were mucking around. It was nothing."

"Yeah, but that wasn't what started it. There have been rumours going round all day. People are saying you and him are together and that's why you split up with Amy… because you're secretly gay."

Olly's stomach turned over as he tried to work out how Scott would respond to that accusation. He'd deny it, of course, because he wasn't gay—more's the pity—but would he be disgusted? Angry? Horrified?

"It's total bullshit," Olly finally said, trying to keep his voice firm and not sound like he was freaking out. "Who started the rumour? Let me guess… Amy? She just wants to massage her ego by blaming the break-up on a sexual identity crisis rather than on the fact that I wasn't into her."

"Yeah I think it was Amy. But other people were saying stuff too. They've noticed you're suddenly hanging out with him all the time, and driving to school together and stuff. You can see why people would be suspicious." He lowered his voice; his gaze was earnest as he continued. "So I thought there was a chance it might be true. Like I said. If you are gay… or bi, or whatever, I don't care, and Olly seems like a good guy."

Olly let out a shaky chuckle. "Yeah, he's great. But seriously, Marty. We're mates, that's all. So do me a favour and spread that around to counteract Amy's lies, yeah?"

"Sure thing."

"Okay. Thanks, man. I've got to go. See you tomorrow."

Olly turned, head reeling and heart pounding as he walked down the corridor. Had he been convincing enough to quell any gay rumours about Scott? Even though the denial was true, the words has been like ashes clogging his throat.

We are just mates, no matter how much I might wish there was more to it.

With unnecessary force, he slammed through the double doors that led outside, momentarily forgetting his own strength.

Fuck everything.

CHAPTER TEN

Scott raised his head as Olly approached. It was obvious something had riled him by the grim expression on his face and the way he strode towards the car. Scott's heart sank. Had football training been a disaster? Oh God, what if Olly had messed up really badly and he was off the team or something?

"What happened?" he asked as soon as Olly reached the car.

Olly didn't answer. He unlocked the car, got into the driver's seat, and slammed the door behind him.

"Olly, seriously. What the hell is going on?" Scott scrambled into the passenger seat. "For fuck's sake. Are you going to tell me or what?"

Olly turned to meet his gaze. His jaw was set and anxious tension bled out of every pore.

"Amy started rumours about us." He took a deep breath and his next words came out in a rush. "Now the whole school thinks you're gay and going out with me, and that's why you dumped her. Well… apart from Marty, who was actually totally okay with the whole thing by the way, but I told him it was bollocks. So he's going to spread some facts to counteract the rumours. But you know what this place is like. Everyone will prefer the more scandalous version." His voice was bitter.

Scott let the words sink in, waiting for the horror and embarrassment that would eventually flood him.

That *should* flood him. Because he had always been so ashamed of his secret desires and the torch he carried for Olly. Being outed had always been the worst thing he could imagine.

Only… now it had happened, and the world hadn't ended.

"Okay," Scott said slowly. "So that explains what happened with Liam earlier. And I thought Marcus was being a bit pissy with me at the rehearsal just now."

"And why people were looking at us weirdly this morning. Fuck, Scott. I'm really sorry."

"How is this your fault?"

"I don't know." Olly ran his hands through his hair in exasperation. "I guess it's not. But I'm sorry anyway, because I know what dickheads people can be. I got a lot of shit from some people when I first came out—not that you're even coming out. This whole thing is ridiculous. But hopefully Marty will set people straight."

Scott snorted and raised an eyebrow, waiting for Olly's brain to catch up with what he'd said.

"Oh fuck. No pun intended." Olly punched him in the arm.

"Ouch." Scott rubbed the sore spot. "Please remember your own strength, will you?"

"You don't seem very bothered about Amy spreading gay rumours about you around school."

Olly's gaze was shrewd, and Scott looked away, feeling uncomfortable.

He shrugged as he picked at a fingernail, focusing on that instead of on Olly. "Whatever. There are way worse things people could be saying about me. I don't care what they think."

"So you're not worried you'll lose all your het credibility by being seen hanging out with me? If it helps, most of your team didn't seem too fazed by it. Even Liam apologised for being a dick at lunchtime. But you might not have to hang around with me for much longer anyway, if we can work out how to swap back to our own bodies and return to our normal lives."

Scott felt a pang of loss at the idea of going back to how things were before all this. He realised then that whatever happened, getting Olly back as a friend was the best thing that had come out of it. "Like I said, I don't care what they think, and I'm glad we're friends again." His voice came out oddly gruff compared to Olly's usual tenor.

There was a pause. Scott raised his eyes to look at him again, and Olly's expression made his heart skip a beat. There was intensity and tenderness there, and Scott wished he could see it on Olly's real face.

"Me too," Olly finally said. His voice was rough too. He turned the key in the ignition and the engine flared into life. "Let's head back."

"So, how was the rehearsal?" Olly asked on the drive home.

"It was fine, I think. Miss Andrews seemed happy. I fucked up a few lines here and there, but not much more than anyone else."

"And the kissing scene?" Olly's gaze was fixed on the road.

"It was okay. Felt a bit weird kissing someone I don't fancy, but at least Demi's cool."

"You seemed to manage it fine yesterday—kissing someone you don't fancy, I mean."

Heat flooded Scott's cheeks; he was grateful Olly was still focused on driving. "Well, that was weird for a whole different reason. I was kissing myself!"

Only it hadn't felt like that, not really, and he wondered if Olly thought so too.

"So, what's our plan for the weekend?" Olly changed the subject, and Scott was grateful.

"Carry on as we are, I guess? Keep our heads down, try and make sure our families don't notice anything weird going on, and hope for the best?" Scott sighed. "I have a ton of revision to catch up on as well as learning more lines for the play. I think I'll spend most of my weekend holed up in your room studying. Your parents won't think that's too weird, right?"

Olly chuckled. "Nah... well, they might assume you're playing video games or fucking about on the Internet some of the time, but my parents don't bother me much. So, what do you usually do at weekends? Anything I should know?"

"I usually go running, sometimes head to the gym. But you can definitely get away with claiming you're studying and hide out in my room. My dad will never complain about you studying too much."

"I guess I could take your body out for a run." Olly glanced sideways and grinned at Scott. "I'm quite enjoying the superior strength and speed if I'm honest. But I'll give the gym a miss. Not being a gym bunny myself, my form would be crap on free weights and I wouldn't know how to operate half the machines."

"Well, do some abs, squats, and press-ups after running," Scott said. "And there are some weights and a bench set up in the garage. I can't afford to lose too much fitness."

They'd arrived back at Olly's house now. He pulled over and switched the engine off before turning to Scott. "Maybe you could come and give me a personal training session to make sure I do it right? We could even try running together, although I'm not sure you'd be able to keep up in my puny body."

"You're not puny," Scott protested. "You just have a really different body type to me. But you seem pretty fit. So yeah, that sounds like a good idea. Tomorrow afternoon?"

"Yes. I'll text you. Oh." Olly's face fell. "But what about your dad?"

Protective anger buzzed through Scott at Olly's expression. How dare his dad make Olly feel bad? "Fuck him. I get to choose my friends, not him. Let's do it anyway—as long as you don't mind having to deal with any crap afterwards?"

"Nah. I can take it." Olly shrugged. "The fact that he's not my dad makes it easier. Rather you than me. Seriously."

"Yeah." Scott sighed. "Okay." He got out of the car. "See you tomorrow, then."

Olly waved as he pulled away.

Scott watched him go. Damn, he missed driving his car.

When he turned back towards Olly's house, a movement in the next-door front garden caught his attention. Miss Wychwood was there pruning an overgrown rose bush.

"Hello, dear." She nodded and smiled pleasantly. "How are you?"

"Fine, thanks," Scott replied, but a tingle of unease crept over his skin. There was definitely something funny about her. Her gaze was too penetrating, too knowing. He had the uncomfortable feeling she could see right through his fleshy disguise into his soul.

He hurried to the front door, trying to chase away the creepy thought.

Friday evening passed uneventfully. Scott found Olly's family pretty easy to be around; they were nice people, laid-back and casually affectionate. If it wasn't for the constant need to monitor himself to be sure he could pass as their son, Scott would have enjoyed their company. As it was, after dinner he was glad of the excuse of revision so he could escape to Olly's room.

Scott did try and get some work done, but his mind kept wandering back over the events of the day. Knowing his friends on the team had been okay with the rumours about him and Olly gave him a strange feeling of freedom. He'd almost wanted to tell Olly not to deny it, to call Marty off and let people believe it. His only worry was what would happen if the rumours got back to his parents—but how could they? The school gossip mill was impressive, but parents weren't in the loop. His heart pounded as he imagined his dad's reaction. It wouldn't be pretty. But was that reason enough for Scott to carry on denying who he was? He was eighteen now, an adult. Even if his dad threw him out, he could still go to uni. He would have to get student loans anyway. He wouldn't be financially dependent on his parents for much longer.

He set Olly's laptop aside and lay back on the bed, closing his eyes and imagining a future where he came out, where he gave up the pretence of being straight, gave up dating girls. He imagined himself back in his own body, kissing Olly. Would Olly want that? Would Scott be in with a chance if he was honest with him? His thoughts sent arousal tingling through him and a painful spike of longing. Maybe he should talk to Olly… but they had enough to deal with at the moment just faking it in their everyday lives. Scott wasn't sure adding an admission of his sexuality and a crush on his best friend into the mix would help either of them at this point. Perhaps when—he had to think of it in terms of *when* or he'd go crazy—they got back to normal, he'd find the courage to talk to Olly about his feelings.

Scott slept in on Saturday. The stressful week had taken its toll, and Olly's bed was familiar now. He finally woke at around half nine, feeling groggy from the longer night's sleep but blissfully relaxed. He didn't have to rush to school, didn't have to face people and pretend to be someone else. He could lie in bed and just *be* for a while.

He rolled onto his back and registered a familiar warm pressure at his groin, the throb of his morning erection, and the recognition sent an extra pulse of heat through him. He hadn't jerked off this week apart from that one time. It still felt wrong to touch Olly's body that way, but the urge was always there. In bed, in the shower, every time he popped wood at a random sexy thought.

Olly didn't mind when you did it before.

The memory of that conversation made him flush. Had Olly given in to temptation yet? He must have done, surely—they were eighteen-year-old boys, after all. Scott normally masturbated every day, sometimes more than once. His body was used to regular release. If Olly hadn't relieved a little pressure by now, he'd have blue balls.

Scott finally gave in and slid his hand down over the smooth, taut skin of Olly's belly. Olly's hips were sharper than Scott's with less muscle to pad them. The skin there was sensitive, and Scott paused for a moment, stroking with his fingertips before reaching down farther to cup the bulge in his underwear. He rubbed his balls and pressed against the shaft with the heel of his hand, biting back a groan at the sensation.

No longer able to wait, Scott lifted his hips and shoved down Olly's briefs, kicking them off. He hadn't been wearing a T-shirt because it was a warm night, and the covers felt good against his bare skin. His nipples tightened, brushing the cotton. He wrapped his hand around Olly's cock and stroked. The feeling of it in his grip—subtly different to his own—drove him wild. He forced himself to take it slow. He didn't want to rush, in the mood to draw it out. The urge to explore Olly's body and make the most of this bizarre opportunity was too much to resist.

He closed his eyes, allowing his mind to spin a fantasy where Olly was there too and they were lying side-by-side doing this together, back in their own bodies.

Just as he was getting into it, Olly's phone buzzed, making Scott jump guiltily and falter.

"Fuck," he muttered trying to regain his rhythm and get his head back into the fantasy.

But then the phone buzzed again, and then again, and then started to ring. The screen read *Scott calling*.

"Jesus, where's the fire?" Scott snapped, his voice coming out hoarse and a little breathless.

"Sorry. Did I wake you up?" Scott paused a beat too long while he tried to think what to say, and Olly cut in again. "Oh, I *see*. You weren't asleep, just *busy*." There was amusement in his tone, but also a suggestiveness that kept Scott hard and aching despite his embarrassment at being rumbled.

"Fuck off," he muttered. "It's not my fault your dick was in the mood."

Olly chuckled, but he sounded a little strained as he replied. "Yeah… well, I know the feeling. I might have to join you."

His words flashed through Scott like a match to tinder. The thought of Olly doing that to his body was too much. "Yeah?" he managed in a strangled voice.

"Yeah, now you've given me the idea." There was a rustle at the other end, and Scott wondered if Olly was doing it right then. "Okay, I'll call you back later. It wasn't important anyway. Have fun. If you want it, there's lube hidden under the mattress."

"Lube? Why do I need lu—?"

There was a click and the line went dead.

Lube? Scott frowned, then he remembered Olly's joke the other morning about arseplay. *Oh.*

He set the phone aside and reached back down. Bypassing Olly's dick this time, he spread his legs wide and tilted his hips up. Ignoring the wild beat of his pulse and the uncomfortable prickle of guilt, he circled a curious fingertip around the tight hole.

Scott had never done this before. It felt so weird, so scary to be touching himself—not even himself, really—like this. But he couldn't ignore the delicious shiver of sensation that rippled through him from even that light touch to the sensitive skin. Getting bolder, he did it again, pressing into the furl of muscle with a fingertip. It relaxed under his touch and he pushed in harder, then bit back a gasp of surprise and discomfort as he tensed up again around his finger.

The grip of Olly's body was so tight, and it burned a little. It definitely wasn't what Scott would call a good feeling, but it wasn't bad either. Just strange and different. But if Olly liked it, it must be okay.

Lube, he remembered. Lube would help.

Fuck it. If he was doing this, he was going to do it properly. He threw off the covers and knelt by the bed. He slid a hand between the mattress and the base until his fingers touched a little bottle. As he drew it out, his heart pounded as though he'd just sprinted the full length of a football pitch.

After checking the bedroom door was locked, Scott lay back down on Olly's bed. He tried to keep the covers over him, but it didn't work well. To be able to reach, he needed to pull his knees right back, so he kicked the covers onto the floor.

He smeared lube onto the fingers of his right hand and went back to touching himself. It was still a little awkward to reach, but his finger slid in easily with the help of the lube, and *God*, Olly was so hot inside, and the squeeze of his muscles was so tight. Scott wondered if Olly had let anyone fuck him. The thought of it sent a flash of intense jealousy and possession through him. He added another finger and pushed in again, wanting to drive away the thought of anyone else touching Olly.

He withdrew and reached in a little deeper, experimenting with angles as he started to thrust his fingers in and out carefully.

"*Oh!*" He gasped aloud as his fingers brushed a place that sent sparks up his spine in a jolt of unexpected pleasure.

That'll be Olly's prostate, then.

He stroked it again. Jesus, no wonder some guys liked this. It felt fucking amazing.

Mindful of Olly's family in the house, Scott bit his lip to keep back the groans of pleasure that threatened to escape as he worked his fingers in and out, rubbing that incredible spot inside.

Eventually the sensation built, swelling and peaking until he couldn't wait anymore. He tried to stroke his cock, but he couldn't coordinate the movements. Not quite able to fall over the edge without the stimulation to his dick, he reluctantly let his fingers slip free. After planting his feet back on the bed, he finally wrapped his hand around his aching cock and stroked hard.

Scott's hips arched off the bed as he came. His arse clenched around nothing, but he could feel the echo of his fingers inside and he came harder than he'd ever come before, sticky ropes of come splattering his belly and chest as his whole body tensed and released, over and over till he was done.

"Holy shit," he finally gasped weakly.

Hysterical laughter threatened to bubble and spill out of him. Half-exhilarated and half-shocked at himself, he lay grinning at the ceiling as his heart slowed and the jizz cooled on his belly.

When he finally moved to clean up, the phone buzzed again.

It was Olly again.

Mission accomplished, said the words on the screen, followed by a kind of manic-grin emoji and a thumbs up.

It was unsettling and weirdly arousing to think that Olly had been jerking off at the same time as him. Scott wasn't sure what to reply without incriminating himself too much, so he went with a suggestive aubergine—everyone knew it was really a dick—and left it at that.

CHAPTER ELEVEN

Olly knew he shouldn't ask.

He really shouldn't.

It would probably make Scott super uncomfortable and awkward.

But he couldn't help himself. It was all he'd been thinking about since their text exchange that morning and he wanted—no, he *needed*—to know.

They were finally shut away in the privacy of Scott's garage, lifting weights after finishing a five-kilometre run, and he couldn't hold back any longer.

It was probably weird to ask. But it was his body, so maybe it wasn't? Hell, who was he kidding? This whole situation was beyond weird, but Olly had to know if Scott had tried using his fingers after Olly did everything but send him an engraved invitation saying, *Hey, please finger my arse while you jerk me off.*

He looked down at Scott, who was attempting to bench-press something that was probably way too heavy for him in his current form. His face was red and strained with the effort.

"So, did you use the lube this morning?"

"Fuck!" There was a loud clang as the weight landed back in the cradle.

Okay, maybe that wasn't the best time to ask him, but it was too late now. Scott's reaction, the darkening flush of his face, and the way he wouldn't meet Olly's eyes made the answer obvious. "I'll take that as a yes, then."

"Jesus, Olly." Scott sat up and glared. "You practically told me to. So yes, I did. Are you satisfied now?"

Olly grinned. "I don't know—you tell me?"

Scott chuckled, some of his discomfort easing with the humour. "Yeah, I think *satisfied* covers it." He flicked Olly's dark fringe aside and wiped the sweat off his brow with his forearm. "God, you need a haircut. Maybe I should nip into the barbers for a buzz cut next week."

Olly gasped in mock horror. "Don't you dare. If you do, I'm getting your ears pierced."

"Okay, okay," Scott said hastily. "I was just kidding."

They didn't say any more about their morning's solo activity, but Olly couldn't stop thinking about it. Being all hot and sweaty and focusing on his muscles while he lifted didn't help.

It was weirdly narcissistic to be admiring what was basically his own body—for now—as he worked out. But Scott was a fine specimen. Olly didn't hate his own body, far from it, but he was enjoying borrowing Scott's for a while.

Scott was struggling. He kept overestimating Olly's capabilities, but his competitive streak wouldn't let him back down.

"Jesus, Scott. Please remember that I don't normally do this," Olly warned him as he strained to complete a set of forty press-ups. Olly was impressed he'd got past twenty. "You're going to be in agony tomorrow."

"I'll be fine," Scott hissed through gritted teeth.

Olly rolled his eyes and started another set of bicep curls.

They finished up with abs, and Scott held Olly's feet while he did sit-ups until his stomach muscles were screaming for mercy. "Come on, ten more," Scott said. "I know you can do it. I did it last weekend."

"Masochist," Olly groaned, heaving himself up until he was almost nose-to-nose with Scott, glaring at him until Scott laughed.

Just then, the door to the garage opened and there was a surprised "Oh. I didn't realise you had company, Scott." Mr Morgan stood framed in the doorway. "Hello, Oliver."

His voice was icily polite, but the expression on his face said it all. He was looking at Scott as though he was shit on his shoe.

"Hi, Mr Morgan," Scott said.

Olly felt a rush of anger, but he bit it back. "Yeah, we're busy here, as you can see. Did you want something?"

"I'm just getting a screwdriver." Mr Morgan walked around them to a drawer on the other side of the garage.

Olly resumed the set of sit-ups. Rage and adrenaline made the last few easy as he counted down from ten to one. By the time he'd finished, Mr Morgan had gone.

"I'm sorry," Scott said as Olly lay back and panted, an arm over his face. Scott patted him on the thigh. "Seriously, man. I'm really sorry about my dad."

Olly uncovered his face and raised his head off the floor so he could meet Scott's concerned gaze. "It's not your fault your dad's a homophobe."

"Yeah. But I hate it."

"I know you do." Olly let his head drop back again. "Fuck. I'm knackered now. And you do this every weekend?"

"Yeah, and usually at least twice a week as well, depending on the football training schedule."

"No wonder you have such an amazing body."

There was an awkward pause. "Um… thanks," Scott finally replied.

Olly flushed. His verbal filter was slipping again. "Just saying. You work hard for it."

He sat up, pulling away from Scott who still had a hand on his leg. "I guess we're done for the day."

"Yeah. I should go." Scott stood and stretched.

"Well, you're clearly not welcome here." Olly couldn't help how bitchy the words sounded, and he regretted them when Scott winced. He changed the subject quickly. "I guess I might not see you tomorrow. But text me if you need anything or think of something I need to know for the match on Monday."

"Okay," Scott said. "And that reminds me. I'm not needed at rehearsal on Monday because they're not working on any of my scenes. So I was thinking of coming to watch the match. As long as it won't put you off? I feel like I should be there supporting my team, even if they don't know who I am."

"That's fine with me." Olly frowned. "But I'm not sure it will help the rumours about us… you know? I mean, I never normally come and watch any of your games."

Scott shrugged, and there was a determined line to his jaw as he replied. "I told you. I don't care what people think… unless you do?"

"Of course I don't care. Everyone knows I'm gay, anyway. But you don't mind that they think we're boyfriends?" Olly said carefully. "Because you do realise that's what was going around the school on Friday? I know Marty's supposed to be telling everyone it's not true, but if you turn up cheering for me on Monday, I don't think it's going to do you any favours in quelling the gay rumours."

Scott flushed a little, and his throat bobbed as he swallowed. "I'm coming anyway. I want to see you play."

A warm surge of affection rushed through Olly. "Yeah? Well, if you're sure. I'll try and do you proud, then."

Olly saw Scott out before heading into the kitchen to get a snack before showering. Scott had told him to eat something with protein in, so he fixed himself a cheese sandwich.

Mrs Morgan came in when Olly was almost finished. She had a pinched expression on her face, and she sighed as she put the kettle on. "Your father said that Olly was round here again." She managed to make it sound like a question, even though it wasn't, really.

"Yeah." Olly tried to sound casual. "He, uh... wanted some workout advice."

There was a pained silence. "You know your father doesn't approve of you spending time with him."

Olly couldn't hold back a snort. "Yeah, he's made that pretty obvious. Olly's a friend, Mum. I'm eighteen years old. It's none of Dad's damn business who I'm friends with."

He picked up his plate and carried it over to put it in the dishwasher.

Mrs Morgan turned as he straightened up, and she fixed her gaze on him. Her expression was hard to read. "Is that all he is? A friend?" She lowered her voice, as if worried Scott's father might overhear even though the sound of the lawnmower in the back garden indicated he was otherwise occupied. "Because if there's more, you can tell me, Scott. I'd rather you did." She took a step forward and put her hand on Olly's arm. Her touch was gentle. "I love you, no matter what. I just want you to know that."

Olly's jaw dropped. He had no idea how to respond. He didn't want to give Scott's mum the wrong impression, but he was touched by her words. This was the first time he'd seen a supportive side to her and he was glad Scott had at least one decent parent.

"He *is* just a friend," he finally said, fighting down his own disappointment at that truth. "But thanks. I guess that's good to know."

She stepped forward to hug him then, a little stiffly, but when Olly brought his arms up to hug her back, she relaxed against his chest. Olly felt uncomfortable but tried not to show it, letting her hold him for a while. He got the impression it didn't happen often.

Finally he drew away, aware of how much he'd been sweating during the run and the workout. "I need to shower."

She chuckled and wrinkled her nose. "Yes, you do."

But before Olly got into the shower, he went to his room and called Scott. "Hey, it's me," he said.

"What's up? Missing me already?"

"I had a weird conversation with your mum." Olly bit his lip. "She seemed to think there was something going on with us, too—don't worry," he added quickly. "I told her we're just friends. But she was… I don't know. She was really awesome, actually. Said that she loved you no matter what. I just thought you should know what she'd said."

"Oh." There was a long pause. "Wow… that's…. Yeah. Thanks for telling me." Scott sounded shell-shocked. "I never would've thought she'd be so supportive if she thought I was gay. I knew she wasn't quite as bad as my dad, but I still reckoned she'd have issues."

"Well, it seemed to me that she was totally on board. So now you know you have options." Olly tried to make it sound like a joke, but Scott didn't laugh.

"Yeah… I guess you're right. Uh, thanks for calling."

"You're welcome," Olly said, but Scott had already hung up.

Olly frowned at the phone, belatedly wondering why Scott would've given that much thought to his mum's reaction to him being gay, given that he wasn't. The tiniest suspicion unfurled along with a hint of hope, but Olly dashed it away quickly. No. No way. It was just wishful thinking. Scott had been very definite about it.

But that was years ago, a little voice whispered in the back of his mind.

Olly tried to ignore it. That way lay heartache. He wasn't going there again.

140

On Monday morning, Olly woke early with butterflies in his stomach at the prospect of the match. It was only a friendly game today, but he still wanted to do his best and make Scott proud of him. He got out the sheet of paper with Scott's diagrams on it, and he went over them again before he got out of bed, trying to visualise the set plays so he could put them into practice later.

He kept the diagrams in his pocket all day at school and sneaked a look at them whenever he could manage it. Scott went through them with him again at lunchtime as they sat in a quiet corner of the library.

"Good luck," Scott said when they parted ways at the end of lunch break. He gave Olly an encouraging smile. "You've got this."

"I wish I had your confidence." Olly grimaced.

Scott clapped him on the shoulder. He let his hand linger there for a moment and squeezed. "You'll be fine. I'll see you later, okay?" He patted Olly's shoulder again before lowering his hand.

"Okay." Olly sighed, watching as Scott turned and walked away.

By the time the bell went at the end of school, the butterflies felt more like a herd of elephants stamping in Olly's guts. He'd managed to force down some lunch because he knew he needed the energy, but he was in serious danger of losing it again.

He went straight to the locker room to change. Coach expected them out on the field for a warm-up while they waited for the other team to arrive.

Olly was one of the first there, and the other guys drifted in as he changed.

"Hi, Scott," Marty took the space beside him. "Alright?"

"Not bad, thanks. You?"

"Yeah."

"How's your boyfriend, Scott?" one of the defenders called across the locker room, and one or two others laughed and wolf whistled.

Marty jumped in. "Shut it, Wayne. I told you he's not—"

"He's awesome, thanks, and probably way better at giving head than your girlfriend," Olly cut across him. The words had escaped before he had time to think better of them.

Oops. Oh well, Scott did say he didn't care what people thought.

Wayne stared, his face red and jaw slack. "It's true, then?"

Olly rolled his eyes. "Good to know you like to be sure about these things before shouting about it." He refused to be drawn further.

Let them wonder.

"What the fuck was that about?" Marty muttered. "If it's all bullshit like you said, then you're not doing yourself any favours by coming out with that kind of joke."

Olly shrugged. "Fuckers can think what they like."

He could feel Marty's gaze on him as he tightened the laces on his boots, but he ignored him. He needed to focus on the match; all this other shit could wait.

As they trooped out onto the pitch ready to start, Olly searched the straggly line of spectators at the edge of the pitch until he found Scott. Scott was looking right at him, and when their eyes met, he gave Olly a grin and a wave. Olly smiled back, a warm surge of something calm spilling inside him and settling the churning anxiety in his belly.

He caught Marty watching him again with a thoughtful expression on his face.

"What?" He glared.

Marty shook his head and gave a small smile. "Nothing, mate. Nothing at all."

For a friendly game, it was fierce right from the first whistle. The school they were playing against were from the next town and were old rivals. It was end-to-end action for the whole of the first half, with several good attempts on goal, but neither team managed to get one past the keepers. Olly played well, feeling more confident than he'd done in either of the practices. The extra adrenaline from having a few spectators ramped up his performance and gave him an extra edge of speed and skill that was exhilarating.

At half-time they got a pep talk from Mr Buckley.

"Come on, lads, keep pushing. Their defence is weaker than ours. Keep at them, and they'll break eventually."

Unfortunately it was their own defence who broke first, early in the second half. To be fair, it was an amazing shot from the other team's striker, who managed to field a beautiful pass from way down the pitch. He was small but really fast. He dodged two defenders and scored with a perfect shot into the top right-hand corner of the net.

After that, Olly's team redoubled their efforts and attacked relentlessly while the other team kept up a tight defence. Finally they managed to equalise with a penalty for a dodgy tackle in the eightieth minute.

With the score at one all and less than ten minutes to go, the pace was furious. It felt like it could go either way, with the action spanning the length and breadth of the pitch.

Olly's team had the ball and were pushing hard on goal. Liam took a shot, but it was blocked by a defender, forcing a corner with less than two minutes to go.

"Come on, lads, this is our last chance," the captain yelled.

Liam went to take the kick, and Olly was right in the six-yard box, jostling for position. He watched Liam, waiting for his signal. He felt oddly calm, though his pulse was thundering in his ears.

The whistle blew, and when the ball came flying at him, Olly was ready. Instinct took over, and the strong muscles in Scott's legs launched Olly high into the air with perfect timing. Straining to the limit, he closed his eyes at the last minute as he tensed the muscles in his neck for impact.

There was a dull *thud* as his head made contact with the ball and then he was falling, his eyes open again and arms outstretched to catch himself as he fell. He raised his head just in time to see the ball graze the tips of the goalie's fingers before hitting the back of the net.

Lying winded on the grass, Olly stared disbelievingly into the goal for a moment, his heart pounding as the cheers and whoops of his team and the crowd rang out.

I fucking did it!

Then strong hands were pulling him up, and people were hugging him and slapping him on the back.

"Nice one, Scotty."

"Fucking awesome."

Then, from Wayne, "Shit, man. I don't care if you are gay. If you can score a goal like that in the match next weekend, I'll join the queue to suck your dick."

Laughter bubbled up as Olly shoved him away playfully. "In your dreams, mate."

He searched the spectators for Scott again and found him. Scott gave him a thumbs up and a massive grin.

"Come on, boys. Play on." The referee looked at his watch.

But it was nearly over. The other team didn't have time to do anything as Fairfield managed to get the ball and keep possession for the last couple of minutes until the final whistle went.

Olly's team lined up to shake hands with their opponents, who muttered crestfallen congratulations. "Good goal," one of them said to Olly as he shook his hand.

"Thanks." Olly smiled, bursting with pride.

The people who'd watched the game invaded the pitch. A few proud parents patted their sons on the back, and the girlfriends of some of the lads came up to kiss them and congratulate them.

Olly wasn't sure how to behave as he saw Scott approaching. He couldn't tamp down the huge grin that spread across his face, and Scott was grinning too.

"That goal was amazing," Scott said. "Well done." And much to Olly's surprise, Scott wrapped his arms around Olly and hugged him tight, right there in front of everyone. "I'm so fucking proud of you." Scott whispered the words in a warm rush against Olly's ear so that only he would hear them.

"Thanks." Olly hugged him back, making the most of the opportunity and burying his nose into the crook of Scott's neck. "I couldn't have done it without you—literally."

Olly finally pulled away reluctantly. Scott's cheeks were flushed and he licked his lips nervously. Olly was filled with a sudden desire to kiss him, so he backed off quickly. "I'd better go and shower. D'you wanna lift home?"

"Yeah, cheers."

"Okay, see you in a little while, then."

Olly fell into step beside Marty as they walked across the grass back to the changing rooms. He glanced sideways and caught Marty giving him that look again.

"It's complicated, okay?" Olly sighed. "I was telling you the truth on Friday, but not the whole truth." That much *was* true, at least.

"Hey, I'm not judging. Whatever makes you happy, man. What I will say, though, is I've never seen you smile at a girl like that in all the time I've known you. And Olly? Well, he looks back at you exactly the same way—like you're the centre of his universe or some sappy shit like that."

"Really?" Olly's heart skipped a beat as wild, crazy hope flared in his chest. Could his feelings for Scott really be reciprocated? "He does?"

"Totally. Like he's 100 per cent smitten."

"Hmm," Olly tried to fight down his excitement. Marty must be mistaken. "I think he was just excited that I scored."

"I think it's more than that. But maybe you should ask him."

They'd reached the locker room now and were swallowed up in the noise and bustle of half-naked boys and the sound of showers running.

Olly was so distracted by thoughts of Scott that he showered and dressed in a daze.

On the way back in the car, his brain was still mulling over what Marty had said. But how could he bring up the subject? If Marty was wrong, it could ruin their newly rekindled friendship, never mind the fact that they were still stuck in the wrong bodies. They had to cooperate in order to survive. If Olly fucked things up by declaring his feelings for Scott and found they weren't reciprocated, it would be painfully awkward—as well as painful.

"You okay?" Scott asked. "You seem very quiet for someone who should be celebrating."

"Yeah. Just…." Olly tried to think how to drop a hint without saying too much. "Well, what with you hugging me like that in front of everyone—" He didn't bother to mention the exchange with Wayne in the locker room. "—I think people are going to believe Amy's rumours even more now."

Scott shrugged. "I told you I don't care. Let them think what they like." Olly frowned. "Unless it bothers you? Sorry, I shouldn't have assumed. Is there someone you're interested in? Will people assuming we're dating fuck things up for you?"

"No. No, there's nobody—" He just managed to stop himself from adding *else*.

"Good." Scott said firmly, then cleared his throat and added, "I mean… good that it's not a problem for you either."

They'd arrived back in their street now, and Olly pulled up outside his house. He felt a pang of longing. He missed his family, his home, his bed… he didn't want to go back to Scott's house and fake it again. Olly was tired. Tired of pretending, tired of lying to everyone—Scott included. His heart thumped as he tried to find the words to begin the conversation he needed so badly to have.

Scott was sitting in silence beside him, making no move to get out of the car.

When Olly turned to look at him, a muscle in his jaw ticked and he swallowed hard. He opened his mouth, but no sound came out. And then it was too late because Scott was unfastening his seat belt and then opening the door.

"Okay, have a good evening. I'll see you tomorrow." Scott got out and was gone, slamming the door with a thud before Olly could say more than goodbye.

CHAPTER TWELVE

Why don't I care? Scott asked himself for the hundredth time. *I should be freaking out that people think I'm going out with Olly, but I* like *them thinking that.*

That was what it boiled down to. He felt free for the first time in years. He'd basically been outed at school, and it was okay. He was still on the football team. From what Olly had told him, he didn't seem to be losing his friends. Nobody cared much, apart from Amy. He snorted, wondering how she was feeling now her plan had backfired. That would teach her to spread stories about people. It just so happened this story wasn't so far from the truth.

He sighed, staring at the ceiling in Olly's room. The early evening sun slanted in through the curtains, a slash of brightness where dust motes danced.

It was so ironic. Despite the whole school thinking he was gay now—or bi, or into guys, or whatever—the one person he wanted to know the truth about him still thought it was a lie. Scott had come so close to confessing his secret to Olly in the car earlier, but he'd chickened out at the last moment. It hadn't felt like the right time… or maybe it was the right time but not the right place. Scott couldn't do it parked outside in the street with the engine still running. It was a conversation that needed privacy and no risk of interruption. Maybe tomorrow he could get Olly to come round to study again. Then he'd tell him.

But Scott hadn't factored in his dad.

On Tuesday at break time, he managed to get Olly alone long enough to ask, "Can you come to mine—I mean yours—after dinner tonight to study together?"

"Yeah, probably."

"Cool." Scott's heart started to race at the thought of the conversation they needed to have. "Has everything been all right so far this morning? Word about us seems to be spreading fast. Have you had any hassle?"

"No." Olly shook his head. "Not unless you count death glares from Amy and a few of her friends. Most people seem okay with it, if a bit surprised at your sudden interest in dick. I'm getting a bit of piss-taking from your mates, but not in a bad way."

Scott pondered on that during his next lesson, pretending to take notes while he tried to sort out his feelings. If people were surprised, he'd obviously managed to avoid tripping anyone's gaydar all these years. Somehow he felt oddly disappointed by that, rather than relieved. It didn't seem right that he could hide something so fundamental so easily.

He saw Olly again at lunchtime, and they went through some lines together. The rehearsal schedule that week was hectic with the play coming up. He had rehearsals after school that day and the next, with the dress rehearsal on Thursday afternoon in front of a load of kids in the younger classes. The thought of performing in front of an audience was enough to bring Scott out in a cold sweat.

Olly drove him home as usual, and when he pulled up so Scott could get out, he said, "I'll see you later, then—around half seven, I guess?"

"Sure." Scott's stomach flipped with nerves and excitement.

Scott could hardly eat his dinner as he waited impatiently for the time to pass. He kept looking at the clock on the kitchen wall and could feel every tick of the second hand like a beat of his heart.

But half seven came and went.

Scott was back in Olly's room now, alternately checking the time and stressing out over how he was going to word his confession. The longer he waited, the worse he felt.

U coming? He finally texted at ten to eight.

There was no reply for about a quarter of an hour, then finally the phone buzzed with a response.

No, sorry :(

Scott's tension released like a deflating balloon, and disappointment rushed in to fill the space. Bubbles appeared as Olly typed more. It seemed to take forever, and when the next message appeared, it was long.

I just had a massive row with your dad. He was being a git, refused to let me come round and see you. Went on about it being a school night and that I needed to focus on revising. He said I could study alone and text you if I needed something. But it was obvious he disapproves of you hanging out with me. I tried telling him I was eighteen and he couldn't stop me, but he wouldn't budge and eventually I had to back down. I didn't want to make things worse.

"Fuck," Scott muttered. Anger rippled through him and a surge of protectiveness as he imagined the exchange and thought about Olly having to deal with that.

I'm sorry, he typed. *Where was my mum during this? She's out tonight.*

That figured. Scott's dad was always extra hard on him when his mum wasn't around to rein him in.

That sucks. I guess I'll see you at school tomorrow then. Scott sighed as he pressed Send.

It was typical that his father was ruining everything even when Scott wasn't living with him. "Not under my roof" was one of his favourite phrases. Well, Scott wouldn't be living under his roof for much longer. Even if he failed all his A levels because of being in the wrong body, he'd leave home, find a job—any job—and get out from under his father's thumb. He was done with keeping him happy. Scott wanted to be free to be himself.

Scott and Olly spent as much time together as they could in school for the next couple of days. They didn't attempt another evening study session; Scott told Olly not to bother trying. He didn't want to expose Olly to his dad's shitty attitude again. Once he was back in his own body, he'd deal with his father himself—if he ever made it back. In his darker moments, he was starting to wonder if they might be stuck forever. Several times he thought about trying to make his big confession to Olly in school, but there was never enough time or enough privacy for him to risk it. Frustrated, Scott felt like the week was crawling by.

They were both anxious about the responsibilities that faced them that week. On Wednesday lunchtime they ditched their friends and found a deserted classroom where they could run through lines for Scott and tactics and set plays for Olly.

"What if I fuck things up for you and the team?" Olly frowned, picking at a hole on the knee of his jeans. He was sitting on a desk, and Scott was on a chair beside him.

Scott put out a hand to still the anxious movement of Olly's fingers. "Stop trashing my clothes. And you won't. You were awesome on Monday. I know you can do it." He let his hand linger for a moment, wanting to thread their fingers together and take some comfort in the touch.

"But it should be you. If the team wins, it should be *your* moment of glory."

"I feel the same about the play," Scott said, pulling his hand away reluctantly. "That's something you've worked for. Even if I get through it without making a twat of myself—and by extension you—I'm taking something that should be yours. But there's fuck all we can do about it."

"Yeah." Olly sighed. "It is what it is."

Scott frowned, leaning back in his chair. "I still can't shake the feeling that Miss Wychwood has something to do with it. Maybe it's crazy to think that, but it's no more crazy than what's happened to us. All week I've felt like she's watching me. Every time I leave the house, she's in the garden or looking out of her window. And her damn cat is always around too."

"So, what are you saying? Do you think we should try and talk to her? Ask her about it?"

"I don't know. I still don't see how we can risk it."

"Yeah. Fuck." Olly ran a hand through his hair, tugging on the fringe as though expecting it to be longer. "I'm just going mad stuck in your body." He grinned suddenly, cheeky and a little suggestive. "No offence, man. I mean, it's an awesome body in many ways. But life is a damn sight easier when I'm not pretending to be someone else."

Scott could only nod in agreement. "Yeah. It is."

When they drew up outside Olly's house that afternoon, sure enough, Miss Wychwood was out in her garden again. She was kneeling next to a flowerbed, digging up weeds, her cat lying on the grass beside her.

"See. There she is," Scott said. "I'm sure she never used to spend so much time in her front garden. It's like she's using it as an excuse to spy on us." As he spoke she raised her head and gave them a cheery smile and a wave. Scott lifted his hand automatically in response. "It's giving me the creeps."

Olly waved too. "I don't know. She always used to say hello to me before. I'm not sure anything's changed."

"There's just something about the way she looks at me. I feel like she sees me—I mean the real me on the inside, not you on the outside like everyone else does. But I don't know why I think that."

Olly shrugged, still watching her. She'd gone back to her weeding, and the black cat stretched luxuriously in the sunshine. "I dunno. Maybe we'll never know why this happened or what caused it."

"I don't care as long as it stops soon." Scott felt defeated by everything today. The reality of their situation was weighing on him more heavily as each day passed. The idea of losing himself forever, spending his life stuck in the wrong body, living a lie… it made him feel sick and hopeless.

"Yeah." Olly sounded equally despondent.

"Okay. Well, I'll see you tomorrow." Scott opened the door and climbed out.

"Yeah, bye."

Scott shut the door and watched as Olly drove his car away.

When he turned he almost tripped over Miss Wychwood's cat. It miaowed at him and twined around his ankles.

"Hello. What do you want?" he said to the cat.

It was a nice cat if you ignored the creepy, staring part. He stooped and stroked its sleek black head, rubbing behind its ears until it purred.

"He's just a big softie who loves to be petted."

Miss Wychwood's voice made Scott look up.

She was standing in her front garden, with her hands on her hips and that knowing expression on her face.

Scott straightened up and the cat gave a miaow of protest. Standing on hind legs, he put his paws up against Scott's leg.

Chuckling, Scott stooped to stroke him again. "You're so pushy." The cat purred and nudged Scott's hand with his head.

"He likes you, Scott," Miss Wychwood said.

It took a moment for Scott to register her exact words. When he did, it was like being dunked in a bath of icy water. Hair prickled on the back of his neck and his heart raced double time. He stood and stepped closer, ignoring the insistent purring and headbutting from the cat by his ankles. "What did you say?"

Maybe it was a simple mistake. It wasn't unheard of for people for mix up names, especially the elderly.

"I said"—her voice was crisp, like the crunch of dry leaves underfoot—"he likes you… *Scott*." She emphasised his name.

"I'm Olly," Scott managed, although it came out slightly strangled.

"No, you're not." Her wrinkled face rearranged itself into an oddly reassuring smile. "You're Scott. And I know this has been really hard for you. But it will be worth it in the end."

"What… how…?" Scott couldn't find the words to articulate the mess of questions whirling through his head. He settled on the most urgent one. "How do we get back?"

Her smile took on a mischievous quality. "How do all romantic fairy tales end?"

The answer was obvious, he'd even thought of it himself—albeit not seriously.

"With… a kiss?" He frowned and flushed. "But we tried that. Well, not exactly. But we kissed for a play rehearsal and it didn't change anything."

Miss Wychwood chuckled. "Oh, Scott, my dear. It's not enough to go through the motions. Magic knows when the heart is true."

And with that, she turned and walked to her front door.

"Wait!" Scott called after her. "I don't understand. There must be something you can do. If you did this to us, you can fix it."

She paused, one hand on the door handle, and looked back over her shoulder.

"It's not my problem to fix. You have the power, Scott. Every fairy tale needs someone with courage, and it doesn't have to be a handsome prince. Be brave and true to yourself, and all will be well." With that, she opened her front door and was gone, closing it firmly behind her.

The cat was still rubbing itself against Scott's legs. Scott crouched down to give it some more attention, turning Miss Wychwood's words over and over in his mind as he smoothed the soft fur.

"Your owner is crazy," he muttered.

The last things she'd said really sounded like the ramblings of someone with a shaky grip on reality. But who was Scott to judge? Nobody would believe him if he tried to explain what had happened to him and Olly.

Miss Wychwood seemed like their only hope. But what exactly did she expect him to do?

Scott thought of nothing else for the rest of the evening, and he lay awake for a long time turning half-formed thoughts over his head. Slowly his understanding of Miss Wychwood's cryptic advice crystallised, and a plan took shape. If he was right, then they *could* fix this. And if his theory was correct, maybe he could have everything he wanted. Was it possible their story could have a happy ending?

Whatever happened, he resolved to somehow talk to Olly tomorrow. Even if his plan didn't work, he was ready to tell Olly how he felt. He couldn't keep the secret anymore.

As Scott drifted into sleep, hope bloomed in his heart.

Thursday morning dawned warm and bright again. When the alarm woke him, Scott got straight up and opened the blinds to squint into the sunshine. The hopefulness from last night hadn't left him, but this morning it was joined by a healthy dose of nerves. He wasn't sure which part of today was more terrifying: having to play Romeo in the dress rehearsal with an actual audience—albeit ones who would mostly be surreptitiously playing on their phones rather than paying attention—or finally confessing to Olly that he was probably gay and had feelings for him.

He took a shaky breath and squared his shoulders. *You can do this.*

One thing at a time. Dress rehearsal first, and then he'd find a way to talk to Olly that evening.

Scott spent every spare minute of the morning going over his lines. Somehow, miraculously, he'd managed to learn them all in time. It was amazing what his brain could do under pressure. Hopefully that would stand him in good stead during his exams in a few weeks—or during Olly's exams if he had to try and cram two years of Psychology and English Lit in one month.

At lunchtime, he met Olly to run through the lines one final time. They sat under a tree in the shade and went through the whole play from start to finish. Scott only faltered once or twice, and when they finished, Olly rewarded him with a huge smile.

"You're going to be awesome," Olly said. "Not as good as I would have been, obviously." His grin turned mischievous. "But you'll be fine."

"Ugh. I hope so." Scott's palms were slick with sweat at the prospect. It was almost time for him to go and put on his costume and make-up ready to start the performance. He wiped his hands on his jeans.

Olly was sitting cross-legged opposite Scott, and he shuffled closer till their knees bumped. "You okay?" He put a hand on Scott's knee.

"I feel sick."

"That's normal. But the adrenaline will help—just like it does with a big football match."

"I guess," Scott said unhappily.

He covered Olly's hand with his, craving the comfort. Olly flipped his hand so it was palm up and then held on to Scott's. Scott's gaze snagged on the tiny white scar on his wrist. It felt like so long ago they'd made their friendship vow. So much had happened since then, but Scott was glad they were friends again.

"You really will be fine." Olly squeezed his hand. "I bet you'll actually start to enjoy it once you're up there."

Scott snorted. "I doubt that. But I'll settle for getting through it and doing a half-decent job."

"Come on." Olly stood, tugging on Scott's hand to drag him up. "It's time to go." He didn't let go of Scott's hand, though. They stared at each other for a moment. "Jeez. You look like you're going to face a firing squad, not a load of bored Year 7s and 8s. You do realise half of them won't be paying attention to you anyway, and if they are, it will mostly be because they think you're—I mean, think *I'm*—hot." He grinned.

Scott laughed, a little of his tension easing. Olly pulled him into a hug, wrapping strong arms around him and holding him close. Scott tensed for a moment, wondering what the hug meant, trying not to hope too much. But then he relaxed and enjoyed it for whatever it was, resting his head on Olly's shoulder and breathing in their combined scents. They fit together perfectly, as though they were always meant to hold each other. It felt so right—even if they were in the wrong bodies.

Finally, Scott pulled away. He didn't want to, but he'd be late if he didn't hurry, and even a hug from Olly wasn't enough to risk the wrath of Miss Andrews. "I'd better run."

"Yep. Damn, I wish I could come and watch you. Break a leg, yeah? And I'll see you after footy training."

There was an extra football training session scheduled today instead of tomorrow, because Coach wanted them to have Friday off to be fresh for Saturday.

Scott nodded. "Yeah."

The dress rehearsal went well.

Scott fluffed a few lines near the beginning because of nerves, but as Olly had predicted, once he got into his stride, the adrenaline helped him stay focused.

The romance scenes with Demi weren't too awkward; they managed to ignore a couple of wolf whistles from the kids in the audience during their kiss.

By half-time, Scott was exhilarated and finally understood why Olly actually enjoyed performing. It was a good feeling and not completely dissimilar from playing football. He was still part of a team, and they had to work together for a common goal. The thrill of the audience clapping at the end of a scene or laughing at a joke gave him the same feeling he got when spectators cheered a goal or groaned at a missed chance.

At the end of the final scene, Scott found himself grinning like an idiot as the cast held hands and bowed to surprisingly enthusiastic applause from the audience.

After they'd changed and washed off their make-up, Miss Andrews gathered them all together. "Well done, everyone." She beamed at them. "You should be proud of yourselves—you did really well. Now you just need to do it all over again tomorrow and Saturday. Go home, have an early night, and I'll see you all tomorrow evening."

Scott was packing up his bag when Demi came over. "Well done. Don't forget to brush your teeth tomorrow." She grinned.

He chuckled. "Nah. I was going to eat garlic bread and raw onion for dinner just to piss you off."

She wrinkled her nose. "Don't you dare, you wanker."

They walked down the corridor together. "You heading home now?" she asked. "I've got to go and catch my bus."

"Nah, I'm going to the library for a while. I've got a lift back later."

"With Scott?" She raised her eyebrows, and Scott nodded. She smiled. "I think it's so cute that you guys got together."

Scott's cheeks heated and he ducked away from her gaze, letting Olly's dark fringe fall over his eyes. "Yeah." He wasn't sure what else to say.

Luckily, Demi didn't seem to find his bashfulness unusual. "Bye then, Olly. See you tomorrow. Don't let Scott keep you up late tonight."

I should be so lucky.

CHAPTER THIRTEEN

Olly spent the afternoon hoping Scott's dress rehearsal was going well. He was all fired up for football training after school. Full of confidence after his goal on Monday and another good training session on Tuesday, he was ready to run off some of his frustration on the pitch.

It was driving him crazy that he hadn't managed to talk to Scott properly during the week. What with Scott's dad being a dick and Scott and Olly being so focused on preparing for the play, it felt like there hadn't been time for anything else.

Ever since Marty had planted the thought in his head on Sunday, Olly had been looking for signs he was right. Was it possible Scott liked him—like *that*?

They were undeniably friends again, and the rekindling of their relationship had brought all of Olly's feelings for Scott back in full force.

However, with him being in Scott's body and Scott being in his, Olly realised it was way more than just attraction. While interacting with Scott with any sexual stuff out of the equation, Olly was aware of the bond between them. The affection, the history that tied them together—it was a soul-deep connection that went beyond the physical.

Surely, Scott must feel it too. But did it mean the same thing to him that it did to Olly?

Where did friendship end and love begin?

If he was honest with himself, he'd been in love with Scott for years. Albeit in an abstract, hopelessly unrequited way that felt more like a crush on a pop star or a sporting hero than something that could turn into a real relationship. Maybe he was still kidding himself. Perhaps that was all it would ever be.

Out on the field, Olly was fierce. His tension made him unusually aggressive as he fought for the ball in the practice drills where they took turns to try and get the ball away from each other.

"Jesus, what's with you today?" Liam asked after Olly floored him with a particularly savage tackle.

"Sorry, mate." Olly reached out a hand to help Liam up, breathing hard with the exertion.

"No worries. But don't break me before Saturday, all right? And if you tackle like that in the match, you'll get sent off, and then we'll be fucked."

"Yeah, I got a bit carried away."

Liam punched him lightly in the shoulder before backing off ready to start again.

Olly was changed and out of the locker room with lightning speed after practice. He texted Scott as he left.

On my way, see you at the car.

By the time he got there, Scott was leaning against the car waiting for him. He looked up as Olly approached and gave him a smile. The expression made Olly's stomach flutter because the smile was all Scott, even if it was on his own face.

It was still weird seeing himself from the outside. If they were truly stuck like this, Olly wondered whether he'd get used to it eventually, or would it always be strange? "Hey," he said.

"Hey." Scott straightened up.

"How did the play go?" Olly unlocked the car.

"It was good. Miss Andrews was pleased, anyway. How was training?"

"All right." Olly was tired now. He'd pushed himself hard… maybe too hard.

They got in and fastened their seat belts. Olly started the engine and pulled out of the space.

Scott broke the silence once they were out on the road, and his serious tone caught Olly's attention immediately.

"I really need to talk to you later. Can you get out tonight and come over to your house?"

Olly glanced sideways at Scott's profile. His jaw was tense as he glared straight ahead at the road. Olly shrugged. "I dunno. You know what your dad's like."

He'd been a pain in the arse all week, hassling Olly about revision and watching him all the time they were together. Olly felt like he was being constantly scrutinised for signs of gayness—like it was a plague Scott might have caught from him.

Scott sighed, sounding frustrated. "How about you wait till he's in bed and sneak out then? That way he won't know, and you won't have to hurry back. He doesn't stay up late on weekdays. He's always knackered, especially by Thursday, and usually crashes out in front of the TV by half nine."

"Okay, I can do that if you're sure you're happy for me to risk it. What if he catches me?"

"He won't," Scott said firmly. "He sleeps like the dead. Once he's in bed and snoring, nothing will shift him."

"What about your mum?"

"She'd turn a blind eye anyway. She did when I was dating Amy and came in late a couple of times."

"Cool." Olly slowed for a junction. He could still sense the tension rolling off Scott, and it sent a prickle of excitement and unease through him. Why was Scott so insistent on them meeting up tonight? He had to ask. "Not that I'm complaining… it will be cool to hang out with you later, but why can't you talk to me now?"

"There isn't time. It's complicated." The finality in Scott's voice didn't encourage more discussion.

Olly pressed him anyway. "What's it about?"

"I might have worked out how to get us back to normal."

Oh.

Olly blinked, adjusting to the totally unexpected response. He waited for relief to flood through him, because surely it was great news if Scott was right? But all Olly felt was a weird disappointment. Once they were back in their own bodies, there would be no reason for them to see each other so often. Even though they were friends again, Olly didn't think it would be the same. This connection between them would be broken, and the chance to turn it into something more would slip away.

"Shit, really? Okay."

Olly had a million questions, but he knew there wasn't time for them. They were nearly home, turning into their street. Right then, Olly resolved that whatever happened, he was going to be honest with Scott tonight. He was going to tell Scott how he felt, because if there was even the tiniest chance that Scott felt the same, it had to be a risk worth taking. And if that meant Scott didn't want to be friends anymore… well, Olly had survived the last four years without him. He'd have to find a way to do it again.

Olly pulled up outside his house so Scott could get out.

"I'll see you later, then," Scott said. "Around ten? Or later if you can't get out that early. Just text me when you're here and I'll come down and let you in."

"Okay. See you tonight."

Scott gave Olly a tight-looking smile and a nod before getting out of the car.

Olly watched him walk up the path, wondering what Scott's plan was to get them back into their own bodies, and what they would be to each other once all this was over.

Distracted by thoughts of how he was going to confess his feelings to Scott, Olly couldn't settle to anything all evening. Barely hungry because of the anxiety clenching his stomach, he picked at his dinner.

Scott's mum gave him a few worried looks but didn't say anything during the meal. The tension in the room was stifling. Mr Morgan ate in silence, ignoring them both. Olly had no idea how to smooth things over and no inclination to try.

Later, once Mr Morgan was occupied—watching the TV as Scott had predicted—a knock sounded on Scott's bedroom door.

"Come in." Olly closed the laptop where he'd been attempting to work on a Psych assignment.

"My hands are full. Can you open it?" Mrs Morgan's voice was muffled through the door.

Olly jumped up and let her in, surprised to find her there with a mug of hot chocolate and a plate of biscuits. "What's this for?"

"I thought you might be hungry. I noticed you didn't eat much at dinner, but you had football training today, and you need fuel."

"Thanks, Mum." Olly took the mug and plate from her. He was touched at the gesture. "Do you want to come in?" He gestured uncertainly.

"For a minute." She came in and closed the door behind her.

Olly sat down on the bed and put the mug and biscuits on the bedside table. The hot chocolate smelled good, and his stomach growled despite his nerves.

Mrs Morgan sat awkwardly beside him; she clasped her hands in her lap and took a deep breath. "I just wanted you to know I've been talking to your father. He's struggling to accept your—" She paused for a telling fraction of a second. "—friendship with Olly, but I've made it clear to him that he needs to find a way to deal with it. His attitudes are outdated and unacceptable, and his own history is no excuse for not challenging them."

Olly stared at her, unsure how to respond. He tried to imagine what Scott would do in this situation, and he had nothing. He hoped Scott would stare at her like a rabbit in headlights because that was all Olly was able to manage.

She frowned, searching Olly's face for a reaction. "I'm sorry if I'm overstepping by saying anything at all. I just want you to know that if there is anything you want to tell me—in your own time—I'm on your side."

What the fuck was he supposed to say to that? Scott's mum seemed convinced Scott was gay, and while it was great she was supportive, Olly had no clue what Scott would think about it. How would he react?

A week ago, Olly would have denied it, sure it was the right thing to do, but now he wasn't so sure what Scott would say if he were having this conversation. Olly didn't dare hope too much, but he was no longer sure Scott was totally straight, so he didn't want to burn bridges with Mrs Morgan by shutting the conversation down completely.

"Um." Olly cleared his throat. "Well... thanks, I guess. I'll bear that in mind."

She sat there for a moment longer, a small frown of concern on her brow. "Okay, darling. That was all I had to say. I'll leave you in peace." She put her hand on his knee and squeezed lightly before getting up to go to the door.

"Thanks, Mum." Olly said quietly. "Really."

She smiled and then let herself out, closing the door again with a quiet *click*.

Olly waited until he heard the stairs creaking with the heavy tread that signalled Mr Morgan ascending. He left it another twenty minutes, his nerves and excitement ratcheting up with each minute that changed on the clock by Scott's bed. At ten past ten, all was quiet apart from the muffled sound of the TV in the room below. Mrs Morgan was obviously still up.

Dressed and wearing a hoodie, Olly felt like a cat burglar as he crept quietly along the landing. He paused by Scott's parents' bedroom door and listened. Sure enough, he heard the sound of loud snoring.

He stifled a chuckle.

Bloody hell. Poor Mrs Morgan having to put up with that every night.

Tiptoeing down the stairs, Olly winced as they creaked. Even if Mrs Morgan might be okay with him popping out for a while, he really didn't want to have to explain anything to her at the moment. He was in a hurry, desperate to finally be honest with Scott after all these years. Even if it didn't change anything, Olly wanted to say the words, to lay it all out there and see whether there was any chance Scott might feel the same.

The door to the living room was ajar, but there was a loud roar of laughter from the TV as Olly moved silently past. Finally he opened the front door and stepped out into the darkness, closing the door behind him with a careful click.

He took a deep breath of night air and a thrill of adrenaline rushed through him. The street was silent as he set off at a jog; the only sounds were his feet striking the pavement. He slowed down as he reached his house, and it was a good thing because a black feline shape slunk across his path just in front of him, making him jump out of his skin.

"Bloody hell!" He hissed, heart pounding. "Are you trying to kill me?"

He wasn't expecting an answer, but a conversational *miaow* came from the darkness on the other side of the road, making Olly chuckle despite his near–heart attack.

He got out his phone and texted Scott.
I'm outside, let me in.

The front door opened a minute or so later. Scott was there wearing Olly's oldest, softest, most-favourite pyjama bottoms and one of his band T-shirts. It was so familiar but incredibly strange seeing it from the outside. Scott was all rumpled and kind of adorable. It was reassuring to see it was a good look on him.

"Hi," Olly said.

"Hey." Scott stood aside to let him in.

The television was on in the lounge, and Olly felt a pang of homesickness as he imagined his mum and dad in there watching a film like they often did in the evening. Scott led the way upstairs and Olly followed, his heart beating harder with each step. His secret was like a cartoon time bomb, ticking away inside him, red lights flashing as it got closer to zero.

As soon as they were in Olly's room with the door shut and locked behind them, Olly started to talk before they even sat down.

"There's something I need to tell you." He kept his voice low, mindful of his sister in the next room, probably asleep by now. "Before you say anything, before we try and do whatever we need to do to swap back… I need to say something."

Scott frowned. "Um, okay, but you've stolen my line. I have stuff to tell you too."

"Please, Scott, let me talk first," Olly begged urgently. He was worried that if he didn't say it now, he'd lose his nerve.

Scott nodded and went to sit on the bed up at the pillow end.

Olly took a seat at the foot, cross-legged and facing him. "So…." He took a deep breath and kept his eyes cast down, not daring to look at Scott as he spoke. "I've had a crush on you forever, basically. Since we were kids. As soon as I started to realise I was gay, you were more than just a friend to me." He paused and risked a glance up. Scott's expression was one of surprise and he opened his mouth to speak, but Olly ploughed on.

"That night we kissed when we were fourteen, I hoped maybe you felt the same. But then you told me you were straight, and I was crushed. After that, being friends with you was too hard. I had to try and get over you, but I never really did. And now… being friends again this past week or so has been awesome, and I don't want to lose that. But I need you to know how I feel whatever happens… whether we change back or not. And I need to know whether there's any chance you could ever feel the same?"

He finally stopped, staring at Scott and waiting for him to say something. Anything.

Scott's shocked expression morphed into a tentative smile; Olly tried to gauge whether it was one of pity. He wouldn't be able to bear it if it was.

CHAPTER FOURTEEN

Scott's brain tumbled and whirled as Olly's words settled and took on shape and meaning. He felt the smile creep slowly across his face, as unsure and hesitant as he was. Could he really be hearing Olly right?

"Oh my God, Scott. Say something, for fuck's sake. You're killing me."

Olly's pleading tone cut through Scott's indecision, and warmth began to blossom in his chest.

"Well, this makes my confession easier, I guess," he finally managed.

Olly frowned. "What confession?"

"I'm gay, Olly. I didn't realise it as early as you did. When we kissed… that was part of what made me work it out. But at the time, I wasn't ready to admit it even to myself. I tried dating girls, but it never felt right." Scott swallowed hard and carried on before he lost his nerve. "I never stopped thinking about that kiss and what might have happened if I hadn't been so scared. I missed you so much when we stopped being friends. I never understood why you cut me off, but I get it now. And I'm sorry I hurt you."

Olly's eyes were suspiciously bright and his voice was hoarse as he asked, "So, what are you saying? What do you want now?"

Scott's heart thumped hard, and he could hardly get the words out around the lump in his throat. "I want *you*. It's always been you, Olly. I want to go out with you, and I want to be boyfriends. Hopefully we'll end up at the same uni next year, so we'd be able to be together. Can we try?"

Olly grinned and sniffed as he wiped away a tear. "Fuck, yes we can." But then his face fell. "But we might not end up at the same uni if we can't get the grades we need. And how are we going to sort our lives out while we're still stuck in the wrong bodies? Speaking of which… I thought *that* was what you wanted to talk to me about."

"Yes. I did. It's part of it. I know it sounds stupid, but I think all we need to do to get back is to kiss each other."

Olly's brow furrowed in confusion. "But we already did that, and it didn't work."

"Yeah, but that was only because we were rehearsing the play. I talked to Miss Wychwood again a few days ago, and she said a lot of weird stuff. But when I thought about it, it started to make sense." Scott's cheeks heated. He knew how mad it sounded, but he was sure that was the solution. "The kiss has to be a real kiss, not a fake one. We have to kiss each other because we want to, not for any other reason. We need to mean it."

There was a long pause. Then Olly nodded in determination. "Okay. It's got to be worth a try." He grinned and added, "And I want to kiss you—for real. So, what are we waiting for?"

They stared at each other, and Scott could feel each thump of his heart against his ribs. Finally, after all these years, they were back here—and this time he wasn't going to fuck it up. Scott held out a hand. "Come here."

Olly got up on his knees and shuffled towards him, and Scott met him halfway. Both kneeling, they took each other's hands. There was an odd solemnity about it, like this was the final piece of a ritual that had been years in the making. They gazed at each other, and though they weren't in their own bodies in that moment, it didn't matter. Scott stared into his own blue eyes and saw Olly's soul. He licked his lips, sent up a prayer to the universe, and leaned forward to close the gap.

As their lips met, Scott's heart swelled. Olly was everything, all Scott had ever wanted, and this was finally happening. Olly's lips parted, and Scott closed his eyes, deepening the kiss as they put their arms around each other, clinging tight until their bodies pressed together, melding into one. The room spun and they lost their balance, toppling back onto the pillows, still locked in their embrace.

Instinctively, Scott held on tight, knowing they had to keep kissing. He lost all awareness of his body. His lips on Olly's were the focal point, the centre of everything as the limits of his physical form seemed to stretch and expand around him until he lurched back to reality with a weird snapping sensation, like a rubber band pinging back to its usual shape.

They broke the kiss, and Scott became aware of his surroundings again in pieces, as though waking after sleep: the softness of the bed under his back and the hard weight of a body on top of him.

"Oh my God!"

It was Olly's voice—and it hadn't come from Scott.

Scott opened his eyes to see Olly looking down at him. The *real* Olly. Dark-haired, green-eyed, beautiful Olly. The best friend he'd lost and had found again… who was now more than a friend.

"We're back to normal!" Olly blinked. "You're *you* again."

"Yeah." Relief flooded Scott. "I can't believe it actually worked. It seemed so crazy."

"More crazy than being in each other's bodies in the first place?"

Scott huffed out a laugh. "I guess not."

"And all it took to get us back was a kiss. If only we'd known that right from the start."

"But it wouldn't have worked, would it?" Scott touched Olly's cheek and smiled. "That's the point. We had to mean it. Before all this, we were still angry with each other. We weren't even friends anymore, let alone ready for anything else."

"I guess so." Olly grinned but there was a hint of uncertainty as he asked, "So… what, are we boyfriends, now? You haven't changed your mind about that now we're back to normal?"

"God, no," Scott said fiercely.

"Good."

And then Olly kissed him again, slow and sweet and perfect.

Scott was filled with a glorious sense of rightness being back in his own body with Olly in his arms. He was bigger and stronger than Scott remembered from their first kiss, and the scratch of stubble on his face was new. He ran his hands down Olly's back until he reached his arse and squeezed, pulling Olly against him until he could feel his growing erection against his own.

Olly moaned and kissed him harder for a while before breaking away to lick and suck at Scott's neck. He pushed Scott's T-shirt up so he could kiss his chest and stomach, then looked up at Scott from under his shock of dark hair, his lips wet and swollen from kissing. "I really want to blow you. Can I?"

His voice was low and husky and went straight to Scott's balls, adding to the building ache.

Scott's cock jerked at his words. "Fuck. *Yes*."

Olly grinned at his enthusiasm and wriggled a little farther down the bed. He made quick work of Scott's fly and tugged his shorts and underwear down enough to get access to his cock. "You'll need to be quiet, remember."

"I'll try." The knowledge that Olly's family were in the house with them added an illicit thrill—not that they were doing anything wrong, but the possibility of people knowing they were doing anything at all made Scott even more hot and bothered.

Olly stroked Scott with his hand at first, just looking at his dick as he did it. The intensity on his face sent another jolt of heat to Scott's groin.

"You've got a gorgeous cock," Olly said. "I got quite well acquainted with it over the last week, but it's a lot more fun playing with it now I'm back on the outside again. I've been dying to suck it, and you're just not that flexible."

"I'm glad you didn't try. That would be an embarrassing injury to explain to my coach if you'd put my back out." Scott chuckled. But the laughter died in his throat as Olly leaned closer and licked a drop of precome away from the tip. Scott bit back a moan as Olly closed his lips around the head of his cock and sucked him in slowly. Their gazes locked as Olly did it, and Scott nearly came on the spot.

"Jesus," he hissed, gripping the bedcovers in his fists.

Maybe Olly guessed how wound up Scott was, because he kept things gentle and teasing at first. It was enough to drive Scott crazy but not quite tip him over the edge. Eventually, feeling bolder and needing the contact, Scott put his hands on Olly's head and stroked his hair. Olly made a moaning sound around Scott's cock and sucked Scott harder, taking him deeper.

"Fuck, *Olly*," Scott gasped. "I'm going to come."

Olly didn't stop. He made a sound of encouragement that Scott took as permission, but he couldn't have stopped himself anyway. He came with a stifled groan, biting his lip to stop from crying out as he emptied himself into Olly's eager mouth. Olly milked Scott through his climax with his mouth, and then teased the last few drops out with a gentle stroke of his hand so he could lick it away. Scott jerked and made a sound of half pleasure, half protest.

Finally, Olly released him with a smug grin. "Good?"

"Amazing." A tiny flare of jealousy sparked in Scott's chest as he wondered about the other boys Olly had honed his skills on, but he tamped it down quickly as Olly crawled up the bed and gave him a kiss that tasted of his own come, which was insanely hot.

Olly ground down against him and Scott felt him hard against his hip. Scott was filled with a desire to make Olly feel good. He wanted to make him come and feel as amazing as Scott just had.

He took charge, rolling Olly onto his side so he could cup the hard bulge through his pyjamas. Olly thrust into his hand and gasped, "Yeah," between kisses.

Thank God for elastic waistbands. Scott managed to get his hand into Olly's underwear without breaking the kiss. Olly felt amazing, familiar, yet not—all hot silky skin and then sticky wetness in Scott's grip. Scott was overwhelmed with the urge to see more, to *do* more. He broke the kiss and pushed Olly onto his back.

Olly gazed up at him, hair rumpled and cheeks flushed. "You gonna make me come?" His tone was a little teasing, a little challenging.

"That's the plan." Scott was nervous but determined.

"I don't think it'll be hard."

Scott grinned and curled his fingers around Olly's erection again. "It feels pretty hard to me."

Olly groaned at the terrible joke, but it turned into a sound of pleasure as Scott started to stroke him. "God, that's good."

Scott pushed up Olly's T-shirt with his free hand and lowered himself to kiss the smooth skin of his stomach and lick where it was stretched tight over his hips as he arched up into Scott's touch.

Olly whimpered, and feeling bold, Scott edged lower. He let his breath wash over the head of Olly's cock, inhaling the scent of his arousal—so intensely masculine and right. If Scott still had any doubts whether he was gay, they were swept away on a tide of pheromones. This was what he wanted. He'd been kidding himself thinking he could ever be attracted to girls.

As Olly thrust up again, the slick head of his cock bumped Scott's lips, and Scott opened for him. He sucked, mouth pooling with saliva at the flavour, and then lowered himself down as far as he dared. It blew his mind: the stretch of his lips, the sensation of Olly hot and hard in his mouth, utterly different to anything he'd ever experienced before. Yet it felt so completely right. The last piece of a puzzle slotting into place.

Overconfident, he choked as he took more than he could handle. There was a definite knack to this. He used his hand to stop himself from overdoing it and managed to get a rhythm going that had Olly groaning and clutching at his hair. With his other hand, he stroked Olly's balls, remembering how good that had felt when he'd done it while jerking off last week.

"Yeah," Olly muttered, trying to spread his legs wider, but he was trapped by the shorts around his hips. "Shit. Let me take these off."

Scott stopped to help Olly wriggle out of his shorts and briefs. Once free, Olly spread his legs wide, completely shameless.

"Is there something you wanted?" Scott teased. "Because I'm not sure I'm reading your signals right."

"Arsehole."

Scott raised his eyebrows. "Is that an insult or an instruction?"

Olly glared. "Both. You know where the lube is. Use it."

Once Scott had slicked his fingers, he went back to jerking Olly off with one hand while he eased two fingers into him. It was so much easier than it had been when he tried to do it to himself. He found the right angle easily, and Olly's reaction as Scott rubbed over his prostate was one he remembered from when he'd done this last week.

Olly gasped and his muscles clenched around Scott's fingers. "Yes, like that," he hissed. "Don't stop."

"Not planning on it." Scott stroked Olly's cock harder, trying to coordinate the movements of his hands as he imagined how that dual sensation would feel. He was eager to find out for himself one day soon.

It wasn't long before Olly climaxed with a bitten-off whimper, his whole body tensing and releasing as he came all over his stomach.

After a half-hearted clean-up, they lay in a contented tangle on Olly's bed, trading sleepy kisses for a while. A warm glow of contentment settled in Scott's chest.

But as he lay in Olly's arms, thoughts of the rest of the world began to intrude, and anxiety started poking at his happy bubble with its spiky fingers, threatening to burst it.

"I'm going to have to tell my parents." He burrowed closer, hugging Olly more tightly. "That I'm gay… and that we're together." The thought of it was scary, but it felt like freedom too.

"Oh! You've just reminded me." Olly drew back so Scott could see his face; he was smiling. "I totally forgot with everything else that's happened this evening, but I had a conversation with your mum earlier, and, well… I think she's going to be cool when you tell her."

"What happened?"

Scott listened as Olly filled him in. When Olly finished explaining, Scott felt as if a huge weight had been lifted. Knowing his mum would be on his side made him feel a million times better about the discussion he needed to have with his parents. "I think I'm going to tell them soon. I want to get it over with."

"Are you sure?" Olly frowned. "This is all very new. I don't want you to come out to them because of me and then regret it."

"It's not new," Scott said. "I've just been trying not to admit it, even to myself. But I'm done pretending. And I'm coming out for me, not for you."

"Yeah, of course."

"I'm not saying you're not a factor." Scott kissed Olly's cheek again—it was so good to be able to do that. "I don't want to hide our relationship. But most of all, I want them to know who I am."

"I get that." Olly kissed him back, and for a while they got distracted with kisses that turned a little dirty again.

A little later, Olly asked. "Do you think we ought to tell Miss Wychwood we got back okay?"

Scott remembered the way Miss Wychwood had looked at him yesterday. "She'll know." He didn't have a shadow of doubt that she would be able to tell as soon as she saw either one of them.

"Do you think we should say thank you, or buy her flowers or something?"

Olly sounded as if he was joking, but Scott answered him seriously. "Maybe we should. If it wasn't for her, we might still hate each other."

"I never *hated* you. I was angry with you, but I never hated you. Did you hate me?" Olly sounded hurt.

"No. 'Hate' was a bad choice of words. I didn't hate you, but I was hurt after you ditched me as a friend. And I was insanely jealous when you came out and started having boyfriends."

"Join the fucking club." Olly grimaced. "I might not have hated *you*, but I hated every single girl you ever went out with. Even the nice ones."

"Well, you don't need to worry about that anymore."

"I guess I don't." Olly rolled on top of Scott and looked down at him triumphantly. "You're mine now."

The way he said it, all possessive and sure, gave Scott a thrill. He replied, "And you're mine," then threaded his hand into Olly's hair and tugged him down for a fierce kiss.

Afterwards, they gave up on talking again for a while, and Scott was okay with that. They had a lot of lost time to make up and he didn't think he would ever get tired of kissing Olly.

Eventually exhaustion got the better of them, and when they were yawning more than they were kissing, Scott admitted defeat. "I'd better head home." He propped himself up on one elbow to admire Olly, all sleepy eyes and messy hair.

"Yeah. I wish you didn't have to. But I need sleep too. Big day tomorrow for me with the play."

"Of course."

Olly grinned. "But my parents will be totally okay with you staying over another time. Just so you know. We could even put the tent up in the back garden, for old time's sake."

"That sounds awesome."

Scott got up and sat on the edge of the bed to pull his shoes on. When he was ready, they crept quietly downstairs and Olly kissed him goodbye on the doorstep—very thoroughly—before finally letting him go.

When Scott caught sight of a black feline sitting on the garden wall, he wasn't even surprised. He stopped to stroke the cat, who purred and rubbed his head against Scott's hand.

"Your mistress is a very clever woman," Scott told the animal. "Tell her we're grateful."

The cat miaowed but didn't try to follow him as he walked away into the night.

Scott had the uncanny feeling that it understood him perfectly.

CHAPTER FIFTEEN

When Olly woke on Friday morning, it took him a while to remember where he was, and when he did, a bubble of happiness exploded in his chest, making him grin like a loon.

The memories of last night fell into place and his grin spread even wider. He thought about their conversation and Scott's confession, about them kissing, and what that had led to… and heat flooded him. He was sneaking his hand into his underwear to take care of business when his phone buzzed.

Scott, of course.

Want a lift to school?

Olly noticed the time at the top of the screen. *Fuck.* He was running late because he'd forgotten to set an alarm in all the excitement of the night before. He had no time for breakfast now, let alone a wank. He answered Scott's text.

Of course. It's the least you can do now you're my boyfriend.

He added a heart-eyes emoji and imagined Scott rolling his eyes at it.

See you in five minutes, then.

Olly was up and dressed in lightning speed, but was still rinsing toothpaste out of his mouth when he heard the doorbell. He grabbed his bag and ran downstairs.

He opened the door to a smiling Scott, who looked as cheerful as Olly felt.

"Sorry, I slept in," Olly said breathlessly. "Let me get something to eat in the car."

"No worries."

Olly dashed back to the kitchen, grabbed a banana from the fruit bowl and a cereal bar from the cupboard. He paused long enough to give his mum a quick hug where she sat reading at the table. "See you later, Mum."

"Bye, love."

Scott was waiting for him in the car.

Olly opened the passenger door—which felt all wrong—and got in. "I just realised I forgot something."

"What?" Scott frowned and his tone was impatient. "Hurry up and get it, then."

"It was this." Olly leaned across the handbrake, kissed Scott on the lips, and then grinned. "Good morning."

Scott's frown vanished and was replaced with a goofy smile. "Oh, yeah. I forget that we can do that now."

They gazed at each other for a moment, and Olly wished it was the weekend so he could drag Scott up to his bedroom and do wonderful, dirty things with him all day instead of going to school.

"Maybe we should phone in sick," he suggested. "I really want to spend an uninterrupted day with you. Are both your parents at work today?"

Scott's eyes widened. "Yes… but no way! You've got the play tonight, and I've got the match tomorrow. Miss Andrews and Mr Buckley will both freak out if they think we're ill."

"Ugh." Olly flopped back in his seat, disappointed but knowing Scott was right. "Yeah. Damn you for being so sensible. Okay, then, drive."

Reminded about the play, he got out the script and read through his lines while munching on his breakfast as Scott drove them to school. It was nerve-wracking to think he'd be up on that stage tonight after missing the last few rehearsals.

"Are you going to be okay this evening?" Scott asked.

"Yeah, I think so. Going over and over it with you means I know what I'm supposed to be doing in theory, even if I haven't practised it since before the Easter holidays."

Scott turned into the school car park. "We can go through lines again at lunchtime if you like? Make sure you know them."

"Sure. Can we practice the scene with the kissing?" Olly smirked. "I think that's the one I need to work on most."

Scott chuckled. "If you want to kiss me, you only have to ask."

"Even at school? I know people thought we were together anyway… but actually kissing in public is something else."

"I'd be proud to kiss you in public," Scott said gruffly and Olly's heart did a happy flip.

"Okay. Public displays of affection it is, then." Olly was totally on board with that.

"I'd like to come and watch you perform this evening if that's okay. Do you think there are any tickets left?"

"I bought one when I was you, so that I could come and watch *you*," Olly said. "So you can use that one, if you like?"

"Cool."

Olly was ridiculously happy all day. He kept catching himself staring into space and smiling, his thoughts turning unerringly to Scott in every spare moment.

They had Biology together after break, and Olly spent the whole lesson staring at the nape of Scott's neck and wishing he could lick it. The skin was tanned and so smooth above the line of his collar. Olly wondered how it would feel under his lips, and he closed his eyes for a moment, letting his imagination run away with him….

"Oliver!" Mr Brewster's exasperated voice cut into Olly's daydreams.

Olly snapped his head up and saw the rest of the class grinning at him, including Scott.

The traitor—this is all his fault.

"Sorry to wake you. But if you could even try and look as though you were paying attention, I'd appreciate it."

At lunchtime, they got food to eat outside in their usual spot by the field and went through Olly's lines. They didn't act out the kissing scene because Scott's mouth was full of ham sandwich when they got to the crucial moment. But they made up for that with some no-reason kisses once they were done, making a group of Year 8 girls nearby giggle and stare.

After, they lay side by side looking up at the leaves that spread overhead, shielding them from the sun. Scott reached for Olly's hand and laced their fingers together. It felt so good being able to touch in public, having the world see that he and Scott were together. But of course there were still some significant people who didn't know yet—and that thought was like a cloud passing over the sun as it popped into Olly's head.

"When do you think you'll tell your parents about us?" he asked.

Scott sighed, and Olly regretted spoiling the happy moment by bringing up a difficult subject. "Tomorrow morning, I reckon. I want to get it over with, but I don't want them to stop me going out tonight. Given that it's not a school night, it won't be a problem at the moment."

"Do you think they would stop you if they knew about us?"

"Who knows? But I'm not going to risk it." Scott squeezed Olly's fingers lightly. "I want to see you in your moment of glory."

"Ha!" Olly snorted. "No pressure, then." But his heart swelled a little more.

"Are you going to tell yours too? That we're together, I mean?"

"Definitely. If that's okay?"

Olly glanced sidelong at Scott, who nodded.

"Of course."

"I'll probably tell mine soon. Then they'll know why you keep coming over. Can you come back for a while after the play tonight?"

"Why?" Scott's tone was teasing as he asked. "You got plans for me?"

"Maybe." Olly grinned and rolled onto his side so he could lean over Scott and kiss him. "You'll have to wait and see."

The five-minute warning bell for the end of lunch break rang, and Olly drew back. Scott's lips were pink and his cheeks were flushed. He blinked up at Olly. "Ugh. More lessons."

"Yep." Olly scrambled to his feet and held out a hand to pull him up. He kept hold of it after, and they started walking back across the grass towards the school buildings. "Is this okay?"

Scott tightened his grip. "It's perfect."

The adrenaline was kicking in as Olly waited backstage for the performance to start. His back prickled with sweat and he hoped his make-up wouldn't run. The hum of the crowd on the other side of the curtain was like the buzz of a hive. Apparently it had sold out.

Olly had got a lift back to school with Demi because they needed to be there an hour before the performance started in order to get ready. His parents would be there by now, sitting somewhere in the audience. Scott would be there too, and that knowledge was a happy glow of contentment in Olly's chest.

"You got many people coming to watch?" Demi asked.

"Just my immediate family… and Scott." Olly's heart jumped as he said his name.

The smile on his face must have been embarrassingly goofy because Demi chuckled.

"You're so loved-up, it's adorable. So, you guys are together now?"

"Yeah. We really are."

"That's awesome."

Miss Andrews came bustling over waving her arms for silence. "One minute to go. Everyone, hush now, please."

"Break a leg," Demi mouthed to Olly.

"You too."

As soon as Olly was out before the audience, the brightness of the spotlights burned away his nerves. He was barely aware of the people watching, carried away with the emotions of the play. As always after weeks of preparation, it was a wonderful feeling when everything fell into place. Even after missing the last few rehearsals, Olly had been through it so many times with Scott that he knew exactly what he needed to do.

Olly felt the thrill of first love and sexual discovery as though Romeo's emotions were his own—it was easy for him to identify with the young lover. As the tale unfolded, his heart ached for Romeo and Juliet's doomed love. Aware of Scott in the audience, he was struck with gratitude that they had a chance at happiness together. Their future was there for the taking, unlike that of the poor couple in the play. A flicker of unease passed through him as he thought about Scott's father, the only family member who might want to keep them apart.

At the end of the final scene, the lights went up for the curtain call and Olly searched the audience for the face he needed to see. He found his parents and Sophie first and grinned at them as his mum gave him a thumbs up. But then he carried on sweeping the crowd, and finally he found Scott. His face was alight with pride, and he was clapping so hard his hands must hurt. He beamed at Olly when he saw him looking, and Olly smiled back, high on adrenaline and happiness.

Once Olly had changed out of his costume and wiped his make-up off, he went to find his parents. The PTA was serving post-show refreshments, and families and friends who'd come to watch the play milled around with cups of tea while younger siblings tucked into the plates of biscuits.

Olly's mum waved when she saw him, so he went to join her.

His mum gave him a hug. "Well done, darling. You were great."

"Yes, congratulations." His dad nodded his approval too.

"Yeah. You didn't suck at all." Sophie grinned. "And it was way less boring than I was expecting."

"Brat." Olly mock glared at her, snatched the chocolate biscuit out of her hand, and took a huge bite out of it.

As he chewed, he looked around to see if he could find Scott, but there was no sign of him. He took out his phone and typed.

Where ru?

Scott replied straightaway.

I didn't hang around. But I'll come round to yours later. Text me when you're back.

Once his parents had finished their tea, they drove home. Olly texted Scott as soon as he was through the front door.

I'm back.

Scott replied. *b there in a few.*

Olly sat on the arm of the sofa, half watching the TV with his parents while waiting for the doorbell to ring. As soon as it rang, he jumped up.

"You expecting someone?" His mum raised her eyebrows.

"Scott."

"I noticed he was at the play earlier," she said.

"Yeah."

But Olly didn't have time to chat. Scott was waiting.

"You were awesome," Scott said as soon as Olly opened the door.

"Thanks." Olly grabbed Scott's hand and pulled him inside.

Still buzzed from the performance, he was excited and impatient to get Scott alone. The day had gone way too slowly. He led Scott straight up to his room, and as soon as they were inside, he locked the door, pushed Scott up against it, and kissed him hungrily until they were both breathless and hard. They stumbled over to the bed, and Olly pulled Scott down in a clumsy tangle. Lips still locked, they got each other's cocks out so they could stroke each other as they kissed. Things got sticky with precome fast, and they swallowed each other's sounds as their excitement built.

When Olly sensed Scott was close, he wriggled down the bed. He grinned up at Scott. "Less clean-up this way," he said, before taking him in his mouth.

Scott's chuckle turned into a quiet moan as Olly sucked him deep. "Oh, that's good. But hang on… can we try something? Turn around—then I can suck you too."

Olly wasn't going to say no to an offer like that. He moved so they were top to tail, and when Scott closed his lips around Olly's cock, Olly's moan was stifled by his own mouthful of dick. It was the ideal way to get off when you needed to be quiet.

It wasn't long before Scott came, and the pulse of Scott's dick in his mouth and the taste of his come sent Olly over the edge right after. It was only then—too late—that Olly remembered Scott was new to this. He looked up to see Scott flushed and wiping his mouth.

"Sorry," Olly said. "I should have checked you were okay to swallow."

"I didn't get much choice in the matter. It was swallow or drown." Scott chuckled. "But it's fine. Like you say—less mess this way. And it was hot too."

Once Olly had turned around again, they lay in each other's arms. A deep sense of contentment enfolded Olly. He was so lucky. This was everything he'd wanted since he was old enough to understand his feelings. It was so much more than a crush, and even though it might be too early to say it out loud, he knew he loved Scott. This wasn't Shakespeare's version of love in Romeo and Juliet—the temporary insanity of new passion. Olly always suspected that Romeo and Juliet might never have lasted, anyway. They were virtual strangers who never had a chance to get to know each other. With him and Scott, it was the real thing. Something deeper, based on knowing a person's soul and not just appreciating the body that housed it.

"So… are you going to come and watch the match tomorrow?" Scott asked.

The hesitance in his tone made Olly frown and draw back so he could read his expression. "Yeah. I was planning on it, but I won't if you don't want me to. Will it be awkward if your parents are there?"

"No," Scott said quickly. "I don't even know if my parents will still be coming after I tell them about us. Well, my mum will, but I'm not so sure about my dad." His face clouded with hurt. "But I do want you to come. Definitely. It's just you hadn't mentioned it, so I wasn't sure…."

Olly shrugged. "I guess I'd assumed. I mean… that's what people do, isn't it? Support their boyfriends. Oh my God, does this make me a WAG? Or a HAB, I guess. Do they have those?"

Scott chuckled. "I'm sure some footballers do, but given that most of them are in the closet, I don't know if anyone has used that acronym yet."

"Well, whatever you want to call me, I'll be there cheering you on. I can't wait to see you play."

"Thank you." Scott smiled and kissed Olly again. "But speaking of the match, I'd better go and get a good night's sleep ready for the big day."

Even though it was tempting to try and persuade Scott to stay a little longer, Olly resisted the urge. It was long past eleven now, and Olly was tired too. Instead he saw him out and kissed him on the doorstep. "See you tomorrow. Sleep well."

"You too."

Olly watched him walk up the street until the night swallowed him. When he closed the door he was still smiling.

CHAPTER SIXTEEN

For a moment, Scott didn't know where he was when he woke up on Saturday morning. His bed smelled wrong and his room was too bright.

He opened his eyes and blinked, everything falling into place as he looked around his bedroom. *His* bedroom, not Olly's. A smile spread over his face as he recalled the events of the last couple of days. He stretched luxuriously, revelling in the sensation. Until he'd spent time in someone else's skin, he'd never appreciated the connection between mind and body before. It was something he'd always taken for granted, but now there was a sense of rightness at being in his own skin again.

He reached down to idly palm his morning erection, happiness and excitement flooding him at the memory of Olly's mouth on him the night before. But then he heard the muffled sound of his father's voice downstairs, and it doused away the contentment as effectively as a bucket of icy water.

Scott's heart thumped hard as he imagined the conversation he needed to have with them.

Fuck it.

He got out of bed and pulled on a pair of shorts and a T-shirt. There was no time like the present, so he gathered his courage as he descended the stairs. He could hear both his parents talking in the kitchen. There was never going to be the perfect time to tell his dad. Maybe he should tell his mum first? But that was just putting off the hard part. He'd still have to do it eventually, and he wanted to get it over with.

His parents were sitting at the kitchen table and they looked up in surprise as he entered.

"Morning, darling," his mum said with a smile. "You're up early."

His dad acknowledged his presence with a nod before taking another mouthful of cereal.

Scott didn't know what time it was. "Am I? Yeah. Well, I was awake." His heart skittered madly and a jolt of adrenaline made his legs feel wobbly. "There's something I have to tell you."

Something in the tone of his voice must have given him away because his dad's head snapped up. Something like fear showed on his face as he stared at Scott. Scott looked at his mum, praying he'd see support. She gave him a tense smile.

"Go ahead, Scott." Her voice was soft and reassuring.

Scott hoped Olly was right and that what he said next wasn't going to be a shock for her.

"I'm gay." The words burst out of him, so easy to say but changing everything. And just like that, his secret was out, and he couldn't take it back even if he wanted to.

He was still looking at his mum, searching her face. Her eyes were bright with tears, but her smile widened. "Thank you for telling us. I'm proud of you, and I love you." She stood up and came over to pull him into a hug.

"I love you too," Scott choked out against her shoulder.

He finally dared to look at his father. His dad's face was expressionless, like carved stone.

Scott pulled away from his mum. "Dad?"

The word came out sounding like a sob. He cleared his throat. The urge to say sorry was strong, but he held it back, refusing to apologise for something he was no longer ashamed of. "Say something, please."

"How can you be sure? It might only be a phase. Young people experiment sometimes."

"It's not a phase, Dad. I've known for a long time at some level… but I didn't want to admit it, even to myself." *Because of you*, he stopped himself from adding. It wouldn't help. "But I'm completely sure."

"Is this because of that boy?"

The edge of derision in his father's voice made Scott's temper rise, furious and defensive. "He's got a name. And yes, this is because of Olly…. Well, not entirely. I'd be gay whether he existed or not. But he's why I'm coming out. He's my boyfriend now, and he's really important to me."

He paused, and his father was silent. So Scott ploughed on, determined. "I'm eighteen, I'm an adult now, and you can't stop any of this. I'd rather have your blessing, but if you can't be happy for me, that's not going to change anything. I'll be leaving home at the end of the summer."

His father sighed heavily. He didn't seem angry, more… resigned, maybe. As if he'd seen this coming and knew he had no more control over this than he did the weather or the passing of time.

"Okay, then," his dad said simply. He shrugged. "You're right, I can't stop you. I'd be lying if I said I was happy for you… but maybe I'll get used to it eventually."

Scott's mum spoke again, addressing his dad. "You'll find a way." There was a thread of steel in her voice. "It's what you signed up for when you became a parent. Unconditional love."

A fierce surge of love for his mother took Scott's breath away. "Thanks, Mum."

"Olly's a fine young man," she said. "I always liked him. I was sorry when you stopped being friends."

His dad didn't say anything else. It seemed that the conversation was over—for now.

Scott's hands were shaking and he felt weak as the surge of adrenaline passed. He was choked and tearful, but relieved that it hadn't been a total disaster.

He needed to see Olly.

"I'm going out for a while," he said.

His mum nodded. "Okay." She followed him to the front door and hugged him again before he left. "Your father will come round. He loves you. He just needs time." Scott nodded, not trusting himself to speak now. "See you later, dear." She closed the door behind him.

Scott was halfway down the road to Olly's house when he realised he had bare feet and had left his phone at home. He still didn't know what time it was, but the sun was low in the sky and a morning mist hung in the air.

He rang Olly's doorbell, hoping they weren't all having a lie-in, and was relieved when Olly's mum let him in almost immediately.

"Morning, Mrs Harper. Is Olly up yet? I need to see him." His voice was rough, and she looked at him curiously.

"He's not. I think he was up late last night"—she gave him a knowing look—"but you can go and wake him."

Scott flushed, wondering what she was thinking. "Thank you."

As he reached the bottom step, she said, "Scott?"

"Yes?" He turned to look at her again.

"I don't know what happened between you when you were younger, or what exactly is going on now, but… please don't mess him around. I don't want to see him hurt again."

"I… uh." Scott wasn't sure how to answer that. Olly wasn't the only one who'd been hurt in the past. "I think we're finally on the same page now. It took a while."

"Well that's good. I'm glad to hear it. You two were always so close." She gave him a small smile and jerked her head towards the stairs. "Go on up."

Once he was upstairs, Scott tapped on Olly's bedroom door, but there was no response, so he opened it. Olly was an unresponsive lump under the covers. Grinning, Scott closed the door quietly behind him and went to sit on the edge of the bed.

"Good morning, Sleeping Beauty." He touched Olly's dark hair, the only part of him that was visible.

"Mmph." Olly grunted and rolled onto his back. He opened his eyes and blinked blearily at Scott. "Whassup?"

The sight of him all sleep-rumpled with pillow creases on his face made something warm unfold in Scott's chest.

"Oh, nothing much. I just came out to my parents, is all."

"Oh my God." Olly jerked upright, his eyes wide. "Already? How did it go? Tell me everything."

"My mum was amazing. My dad was—" Scott sighed. "—difficult. But it could have been worse. He's not throwing me out or anything, but I think we're going to need to hang out here a lot for the rest of the summer if it's okay with your parents. My dad didn't actually use the words 'not under my roof,' but it will be uncomfortable for all of us if we spend much time there."

"That's fine. My parents will be totally cool with it—once I've told them, of course. They might even let you stay over in my room. We're both eighteen, after all."

"That would be—" *Weird* was Scott's first thought. But once they got used to it, it would be awesome too. He liked Olly's family, and if they were cool with their relationship, then Scott would embrace that. "That would be great."

The idea of waking up with Olly beside him was definitely appealing. He leaned forward to kiss him, aiming for his lips, but Olly ducked away, so Scott got his cheek instead.

"No fair. I haven't brushed my teeth."

"I don't care." Scott put a hand on his chin and turned his head back. "And I haven't either, because I haven't had breakfast yet." He kissed Olly properly then, a soft press of lips that felt so right.

When they separated, Olly's grin was blinding, reflecting back Scott's happiness. "Want to go and get some breakfast now?"

"Yeah. I'm starving."

Scott watched as Olly climbed out of bed, and he admired the lean stretch of his body as Olly stooped to pick up his jeans from the floor and then stepped into them. A thrill of arousal rippled through Scott as he remembered what they'd done last night and the night before. He couldn't wait to try more things with Olly. His imagination spun off with various possibilities.

Olly straightened up with his hands on his hips and a hungry look in his eyes that had nothing to do with breakfast. "If you don't stop looking at me like that, you won't be getting fed anytime soon."

"Food is overrated." Scott stood and crossed the gap. Putting his hands on Olly's hips, he hauled him close for a kiss that was deep and dirty. Olly melted against him, and Scott could feel him getting hard.

Just then, a loud knock on the door made them jump apart guiltily.

"Mum told me not to barge in." Sophie's voice came loudly through the door. "But Dad's making pancakes, and he wants to know if you and Scott want some?"

Olly raised his eyebrows at Scott, who nodded. The mood was broken now, and pancakes sounded awesome.

"Yes, please," Olly called back. "We'll be down in a minute." He kissed Scott lightly once more, then broke away to put a T-shirt on.

"I think your mum's guessed something's going on with us," Scott said. "I got the impression she knew I was here late last night."

"She has spidey senses like that." Olly's head emerged from the neck of his T-shirt, hair even messier than before. He ran his hands through it. "We need to tell them anyway. If that's all right?"

Scott nodded. No more secrets. It would be nice to have Olly's family knowing about them. "Come on, then."

They went downstairs together, and Olly took Scott's hand in the hallway, linking their fingers together. "Is this okay?"

Scott squeezed his hand. It was more than okay. It was wonderful. "Yeah, of course."

The kitchen was noisy chaos. Mr Harper was standing over a sizzling pan and the smell of not-quite-burning butter was strong. Sophie and Mrs Harper were sitting at the table chopping fruit. Sophie didn't look up as they came in; she was wearing headphones and swayed in time to an inaudible beat. Mrs Harper greeted them, and a smile spread over her face when her gaze dropped to their joined hands.

"I've got some news," Olly said breezily. "Me and Scott are boyfriends now."

"That's wonderful," Mrs Harper said.

"About time," Mr Harper grinned at them from his spot at the cooker. "We were expecting this years ago."

Scott flushed, but Olly just laughed. "Better late than never." He let go of Scott's hand, slid his arm around Scott's waist, and kissed his cheek.

Scott's face flamed at the casual display of affection, but his heart soared.

Sophie finally raised her head and took out one of her earbuds. "Wow. What did I miss? Oh. So the rumours at school were true, then? Congrats." She put her earbud back in and went back to chopping bananas.

"Well, now we've got that out of the way, can we help with breakfast?"

"I think nearly everything is done," Mr Harper replied. "I guess that puts you boys on washing-up duty."

After breakfast—which was delicious—Scott helped Olly clear up. Olly's parents had retreated to the garden with coffee, and Sophie disappeared to her room.

"What do you want to do for the rest of the morning?" Scott asked as he put the frying pan in the drying rack. "I could do with kicking a football around in the park for a while. I'm out of practice—mentally, at least."

"I could help with that." Olly closed the dishwasher where he'd stacked the dirty plates.

Scott poured washing-up water away. "Sounds good. Let's jog there, have a kick around, and then walk back."

"This feels like the last bit of fun we'll get to have for a while." Olly sighed. "Once this weekend is over, it's going to be nothing but revision from now till our exams." He handed the tea towel to Scott so he could dry his hands.

Scott's stomach flipped with nerves at the thought. "Yeah. But we have to do it. We need to get good grades so we can be together next year."

"That's a great incentive, at least. And we can revise together, maybe?" Olly sounded hopeful.

"As long as we don't distract each other."

Olly grinned suggestively. "We can take regular breaks. Orgasms are very good for stress relief, so really we'd be helping ourselves to focus. It's a sensible strategy."

Scott chuckled. "Of course. Maybe we can start on that later this morning after you've gone through your lines?"

"Yes, please." Olly put his arms around Scott and kissed him. Sweet, but with a hint of sexy too.

Scott went back to his house at around midday. He ought to get some lunch to fuel himself for the match this afternoon, but he heard his parents talking in the kitchen. His father's voice was raised, so he went straight up to his room. The last thing he needed was to walk in on an argument.

He sat at his desk and tried half-heartedly to focus on some revision but was distracted by the intermittent sound of heated discussion from the kitchen below. He couldn't make out the words, but eventually things quietened down.

There was a knock on his door.

"Come in," Scott said warily.

It was his mum. "I thought I heard you come in," she said brightly. "I know you won't want a big meal with the match soon, but I'm making sandwiches for your dad and me, so I can do one for you if you like?"

"Can I eat it in my room? Dad doesn't sound like he'll be good company at the moment."

She sighed. "You're going to have to face each other sometime, you know."

Scott felt a flash of irritation. "He's the one with the problem, not me."

"Exactly. So you shouldn't be hiding away in your room. You have nothing to be ashamed of. And he knows that, really. He's just finding it hard to accept, but he'll get there. Come down and eat with us."

"Okay." Scott sighed. He knew she was right. The only way he and his dad were going to get past this was by trying to be normal around each other.

His mum's face broke into a smile of relief. "Good. I'll call you when it's ready. Is ham and cheese with salad okay for you?"

"Yes, thanks."

Lunch started predictably with Scott and his dad exchanging awkward nods in greeting. But his mum chattered away and asked them both questions until the conversation started to flow—mostly about Scott's exams and revision schedule, but it beat sitting there in uncomfortable silence.

"What time do you need to leave for the match?" His dad asked suddenly, looking up at the kitchen clock.

"By one," Scott said. "Coach wants us there to warm up at one fifteen.

"We'd better get a move on, then. Go and get your kit. We'll take my car."

Scott swallowed nervously. "Uh, okay. I was going to drive myself. I thought you'd probably come later." He'd assumed that even if his parents were coming to watch, they'd make their own way there in time for the kick-off at two o'clock—and he'd already told Olly he'd give him a lift.

"No. It seems daft taking two cars if we don't need to," his dad replied with a shrug.

Scott took a fortifying breath and met his dad's gaze without flinching. "Well, in that case, can we get Olly on the way? He's coming to watch too, and I was going to drive him."

There was a brief moment of silence as Scott's heart pounded hard. A shadow of a frown crossed his father's face but was gone almost as soon as Scott saw it.

"Yes, of course," his mum chipped in, her voice breezy. "That's fine isn't it, dear?" She glared at Scott's dad, who cleared his throat.

"Yes. Yes, of course."

Ugh. Well at least they were going to get this over with. Scott knew it was going to be difficult the first time his dad had to see him and Olly together. It was probably better to get it out of the way, but he could do without this stress before the match when he was already nervous.

"I'll go and get changed, then."

Up in his room, Scott texted Olly to warn him they'd be travelling with his parents.

Olly replied with a *Yikes!* and then quickly added, *I promise not to grope you in the back seat.*

That made Scott laugh and his nerves lifted a little.

When they got to Olly's house, Scott didn't need to get out to knock on his door because Olly was already waiting on the doorstep. He ran over to the car and got in, giving Scott a huge smile as he slid into the seat beside him.

"Hi, Mr and Mrs Morgan. Thanks for the lift," he said as he strapped himself in.

"Hello, Olly." Scott's mum's voice was warm and friendly.

"No problem," Mr Morgan replied gruffly.

At least he was being civil.

On the back seat, the space between Scott and Olly felt too big. Scott's fingers were itching to reach for him, but he didn't want to make things more awkward than they already were.

When they got to school, Scott felt bad about having to leave Olly with his parents in order to go and find his team. "Okay, I'll see you guys later, then," he said.

"Good luck, darling," his mum said.

Olly gave him an encouraging grin. "You'll be awesome."

Scott wanted to hug him, but he was too aware of his father watching them. "Thanks. I hope so."

Scott shouldered his bag and walked off towards the changing rooms to find his teammates.

Once they all assembled, the coach had them out to run a few laps of the pitch and stretch before kick-off.

There was an almost-carnival atmosphere among the spectators who lined the edge of the pitch. Being a home game, lots of family and friends had come to watch. It was rare to have a school game scheduled at a weekend, and the team weren't used to having many people supporting them. There was even a half-arsed banner painted on a sheet reading "Go Fairfield!"

It only added to Scott's tension. He didn't want to let them down. Olly stood with his parents, and Scott relaxed a little when he saw him chatting to his mum and looking perfectly relaxed. His dad stood off to the side with his hands in his pockets. He caught Scott looking at him and gave him a nod and a half-smile.

Right from the first whistle, the match was fiercely competitive. Both teams were hyped up and desperate to win.

Scott was enjoying himself; it felt great to be out on the pitch again. But an early error on the part of the defenders on the Fairfield team meant their opponents scored the first goal. Fairfield upped their game and fought hard to try and equalise, but they couldn't get through their opponents' ironclad defence. Despite his frustration, Scott had to admire how well they were playing. At the forty-minute mark, a careless tackle by one of the defenders on his team gave away a penalty that their goalie, Jack, couldn't keep out. They went into half-time 2–0 down and feeling despondent.

The coach did his usual pep talk, refusing to let them dwell on the failures of the first half.

"You can do this. Yes, their defence are good, but so are you." He glared at his attackers. "I know you have it in you. Close your eyes, imagine that ball hitting the back of the net, imagine the cheers. Do it!"

One or two of the boys sniggered, but Coach glared at them till they complied. Scott took a deep breath. In his mind he was holding his fist up in victory as he put an awesome shot past the goalie.

A sharp clap of the coach's hands brought him back to the sweaty locker room.

"Now go out there and make it happen."

They went into the second half with renewed energy. The other team's defence were still tight, but as Scott and the other attackers kept up the pressure, chinks began to show in their armour. Finally, Scott managed to make it 2–1 at seventy-five minutes, with a lucky long shot from at least twenty-five metres out. He put it high into the top left-hand corner of the net, and the goalie couldn't get to it.

Scott's team swarmed around him, patting him on the back and yelling in delight. When he glanced at the sidelines, he saw Olly jumping up and down and clapping. His parents were clapping too—albeit in a more restrained way.

"Come on, back to it. We need two more like that."

The next goal came from a corner and was a beautiful header from Liam to equalise with just ten minutes to go.

After that, it was furious action. Both teams were pushing as hard as they could for that all-important deciding goal. Scott nearly had a heart attack when the ball got through their defence and the star striker on the other team had a perfect chance to score. But Jack did an amazing dive for the ball and miraculously deflected it for a corner. Then Jack caught the ball from the corner kick and sent it flying back up to the other end. Liam got the ball out on the left wing and Scott put on a huge burst of speed, timing his run perfectly to connect with Liam's pass and praying he wasn't offside. The defence were behind him now, caught on the hop by the sudden attack. Acting on pure instinct, Scott took the shot. The goalie dived for it… but didn't get there in time.

The sight of the ball hitting the back of the net was the best thing he'd ever seen. Yet despite the raucous cheers of the rest of his team and the supporters, he didn't dare believe it until he checked the linesman's flag and saw it had stayed down.

Thank fuck.

At 3–2 with five minutes to go, the seconds crawled by. The other team had nothing to lose now, so they threw everything at the goal. All their defenders were up, trying for a moment of glory. At the final corner, even their goalie came up to help. But it wasn't enough. The final whistle went and Scott nearly collapsed with relief and elation as cheers rang out from their supporters, and his team crowded around him in a sweaty hug pile, yelling in delight.

When Scott finally extracted himself from the throng, the first person he looked for was Olly. When Olly saw him looking, he raised his hands over his head, still clapping.

Wild joy tore through Scott: pride at winning and elation at having Olly there to see it. Not caring what anyone thought, he sprinted across the pitch and into Olly's waiting arms. He kissed Olly hard. Olly kissed him back and Scott could feel the shape of his smile.

"We did it!" he gasped when he finally pulled away.

"I'm so fucking proud of you." Olly's eyes were bright and intense, and Scott didn't want to look away. But he suddenly remembered his parents were there, so he reluctantly released Olly and turned to face them.

"Well played," his dad said, stepping forward to clap Scott on the shoulder. His gaze slid sideways to Olly and then settled on Scott again. "That final goal was a beauty." He smiled, and the tension drained from Scott's body.

"Thanks, Dad. I'd better get back." His teammates were lining up for the handshakes and his coach was beckoning.

He jogged back over to rejoin them. "Sorry, Coach," he said, sheepish.

Coach slapped him on the back. "After that last goal, I can forgive you. Well done, Scott. Right, lads, who's coming to celebrate at the White Horse? The first round's on me, and if you're not eighteen yet, I don't want to know." He tapped his nose and the boys laughed. "Go and change out of your boots, and I'll see you there in ten minutes. Bring your girlfriends if you like—or boyfriends." He winked at Scott. "But they have to buy their own. I don't get paid enough for that."

Scott went back to his parents and Olly after he'd changed into his trainers. "We're going to the White Horse for a drink, so I'll see you back at home later," he said to his parents, and then, to Olly, "Do you want to come to the pub? But you have to buy your own beer."

"I'll probably stick to Coke as I've got the play tonight, but that sounds good."

"I think we should go out for dinner tonight to celebrate your win, Scott," his dad said. "What do you say, pizza? Or the King's Head—they do a good range of food there."

"Well, I'll probably be meeting the lads in the pub again this evening for a longer celebration." Olly would be busy with the play again tonight, so Scott had been planning on going out.

"Tomorrow, then?" his dad persisted.

Scott normally loved the idea of eating out, but he'd been hoping to spend time with Olly tomorrow night. "Um, I'm not sure—"

But his dad interrupted to add, "And Olly, would you like to join us? You'd be welcome."

Olly raised his eyebrows at Scott in an unspoken question. Scott gave a small nod.

"I'd love to, thank you, Mr Morgan," Olly replied smoothly.

"Okay, good." Scott's dad's voice was gruff, but he didn't sound displeased.

Scott's spirits rose even higher. The fact that his dad was including Olly in their plans meant a lot.

"That sounds great, Dad." He turned to Olly. "Come on, then, the others are going. See you later, Mum, Dad."

His parents waved them off, and Olly walked back across the pitch with Scott to rejoin the rest of the team and a few assorted girlfriends.

Nobody questioned Olly's presence as they walked en masse to the pub at the end of the road. Scott felt like he couldn't stop smiling even if he tried. Every time he caught Olly's eye, he grinned wider. Eventually he grabbed Olly's hand and laced their fingers together.

"Aw, look at you two," Marty said, ruffling Scott's hair in an annoying way. "You're so cute."

"Fuck off," Scott said.

But he still couldn't stop grinning, and he didn't let go of Olly's hand.

CHAPTER SEVENTEEN

Dinner on Sunday was a surprisingly relaxed affair. Olly was half dreading it, unsure of how welcome he really was.

During the match, Mr Morgan had seemed uncomfortable around him, not making any effort at conversation. Thankfully, Mrs Morgan had been awesome. But when Mr Morgan had invited him out for dinner, Olly wasn't going to turn down the olive branch.

They'd ended up going to Pizza Express—Scott's choice, but Olly heartily approved.

It probably helped the mood that Mrs Morgan had offered to drive, so Mr Morgan had a few glasses of wine with dinner. It seemed to make him relax and become more sociable, and by the time they were eating dessert, Mr Morgan was chattier than Olly had ever seen him. He seemed to have got used to Olly being there and was including him in the conversation.

"So, what are your plans for next year?" he asked.

"Well… if I get the grades I'm hoping to go to Manchester to study Psychology. I need two A's and a B, which should be possible as long as I work hard for the next few weeks."

"Oh, Manchester!" Mrs Morgan exclaimed. "That's Scott's first choice too."

"I know." Olly couldn't hold back a smile. He glanced at Scott, who smiled back, cheeks flushing. "How's that for luck? We couldn't have planned it better if we'd tried."

"Well, I guess that will give you plenty of motivation to work hard, then." Mr Morgan took another sip of his wine.

"Yeah, it will." Scott nodded, jaw set with determination. "It would be awesome to be in the same city."

"You might even be able to end up in the same hall of residence." Mrs Morgan smiled.

Olly shrugged. They hadn't got as far as talking about stuff like that. "Yeah, maybe. We've been neighbours all this time, why stop now?"

Scott chuckled. "Sounds good to me."

As they were walking back to where the car was parked in the summer twilight, they passed a small supermarket with bunches of flowers outside in buckets and some growing plants in pots. The colourful blooms and glossy green leaves caught Olly's attention and gave him an idea.

"Scott." Olly tugged on his arm to make him stop.

"What?"

Olly nodded at the flowers. "Miss Wychwood?" He muttered quietly so Scott's parents wouldn't hear.

"Good idea. Hey, Mum," Scott called and she turned. "We're just popping in here for something. We'll catch you up at the car."

"I think she'd like something growing rather than cut flowers," Olly suggested. "How about this vine?" He pointed to a vigorous-looking thing with shiny variegated leaves in red and green. Tumbling over the edge of the pot, it was already trying to twine around its neighbours.

"Yeah, I think she'd like that."

They paid for their purchase, and Olly carried the plant carefully as they hurried to catch up with Mr and Mrs Morgan at the car.

Scott's parents looked in surprise at the plant in Olly's arms, but didn't ask why they'd stopped to buy it or who it was for.

"Can you drop us off at Olly's when we get back home?" Scott asked.

"Of course." Mrs Morgan reversed out of the parking space.

By the time she stopped to let them out at Olly's house, it was nearly dark. Olly thanked them for dinner.

"You're welcome, dear," Mrs Morgan said.

"Don't be too late, Scott," Mr Morgan cautioned. "It's a school night, remember."

"I won't, Dad. See you later."

As the car pulled away, Olly let out a happy sigh. "Well, that went about as well as could be expected. I think your dad is almost starting to like me."

"Yeah, it was okay, wasn't it?"

"Definitely. Considering how shitty he was about me before you came out, I think he's made a pretty miraculous turnaround."

"We can probably thank my mum for that."

"Yeah," Olly agreed. He adjusted his grip on the plant pot. "Speaking of thanking people, do you think it's too late to go and knock on her door now? Or we could just leave it on the doorstep with a note."

Scott turned to look at Miss Wychwood's house. "Hard to know. There's no lights on."

"She could be in a room at the back. It's not that late. Let's try. And if she doesn't answer, we can come back tomorrow."

Olly couldn't suppress a frisson of nerves as they approached her door. He was hoping she wouldn't answer. Facing her would be less intimidating in daylight. What if she cast another spell on them? But he reminded himself she'd helped them get where they were now. Without her, he'd still be pining after his lost best friend instead of dating him and going out for dinner with his parents.

He took a deep breath and squared his shoulders, gripping the plant pot tight as Scott knocked firmly on the door. *Rat-tat-tat.*

They waited, but the door remained firmly closed.

"Shall I try again?" Scott whispered. "She still gives me the creeps, though. What if she turns us into frogs next?"

"Shhh." Olly nudged him. "It's fine. Whatever else she did, she was trying to help. Think of her as a fairy godmother."

"I guess." Scott still looked uncertain.

"Go on. Try once more."

Scott lifted his hand, but before he could knock again, the door creaked open making them both jump.

"Olly and Scott. What a nice surprise." Miss Wychwood's eyes twinkled as she looked at them. "I take it this isn't about a football in my back garden this time?"

Scott chuckled nervously. "Um, no."

Olly thrust the plant at her. "We bought you this… to say thank you. I think you know what for."

She gave him one of those looks that made him feel as though she knew far too much about him, but he met her gaze. Her eyes were kind as well as perceptive. He was pretty sure she was one of the good ones—witch, fairy, whatever she was.

"That's very kind," she said finally, and took the plant out of his hands. "There's really no need. I merely gave fate a little nudge. It was nothing."

Privately, Olly thought putting them in each other's bodies for nearly a fortnight was more than "a little nudge." She could have tried something less drastic, perhaps. But he wasn't going to argue with her. It had got results, after all.

"Well… that's what we came to say." Olly shifted uncomfortably from foot to foot.

"Would you like to come in? I could make tea, or cocoa, or I have some lemonade in the fridge?"

Olly glanced nervously at Scott. His face was hard to read, but Olly guessed he wouldn't be keen. "Um, that's kind of you, but we can't stay."

"Yeah, we need to study," Scott chipped in. "We have our exams coming up soon."

"Of course, dear." She nodded, and a hint of something that looked like sadness flitted across her features.

Olly felt bad for wanting to get away. She was probably lonely, and he was sure she was—not harmless exactly, but he believed she had their best interests at heart even if her methods were a little alarming. "Maybe we can visit you another time, if you like?" he said impulsively.

Scott stiffened next to him, but Olly ignored him.

The smile she rewarded him with told him his hunch was correct. "I would like that very much." Her grin turned mischievous as she turned her gaze on Scott and added, "And I can promise that I would *never* turn either of you into a frog, or indeed, do anything to harm you."

"Oh God, I'm sorry." Scott's face turned scarlet.

She gave a cackle of delight. "It's okay, Scott. Don't be embarrassed. You have good reason to be wary of me. But I won't meddle again. You're back on track now. As long as you both work hard for these exams, I think your happily ever after is assured. Now, go and do that revision."

With that, she dismissed them, still smiling. "Run along. I'll see you soon, I'm sure. Good luck with those exams. Why don't you come and visit me when they're over and let me know how they went?"

"We will," Olly promised.

Back out in the dark street, they paused by the gate to Olly's front garden.

"I probably *should* go home and revise," Scott said.

"Yeah. Me too."

Scott bit his lip, looking uncertain. "Do you think she's right about our exams, and... the rest of it?"

"The happy-ever-after part?"

Scott nodded. "Yeah."

"Who knows," Olly replied. He still couldn't decide exactly what he believed about Miss Wychwood. Maybe it was better not to know too much.

Scott frowned. "It's weird to think about, that our future might be all mapped out already."

"Yeah. But it went off course before, so I suppose nothing is ever certain. Still, the idea that I might get to live happily ever after with you is pretty appealing."

Scott's face broke into a smile. "Yeah. I guess it is."

Olly put his arms around Scott and pulled him in for a kiss. He couldn't think of anything better than a happy ever after with his best friend. They'd have to work for it, whether it was their destiny or not. But right then, with Scott's arms around him in the warm summer night, anything seemed possible.

EPILOGUE

Seven months later

Scott woke to the wonderful feeling of Olly wrapped around him, morning wood poking his hip and the tickle of his breath on Scott's chest. Even after a few months of this, he felt grateful for it every morning. Eyes still closed, he tightened his arm around Olly and breathed in the scent of him, of *them*. All warm skin and musky masculine scent, it was comfort and sexiness combined.

They'd ended up living in the same hall of residence and tended to sleep together most nights unless one of them was pulling an all-nighter for an essay deadline.

Back home for Christmas, Scott had braced himself to spend their nights apart at their respective parents' homes, but Olly had insisted his parents would be okay with him sleeping over.

He was right; they were totally cool with it. Scott suspected his mum and dad wouldn't be quite so happy about Olly staying in his room, so by unspoken agreement he spent his nights in Olly's bed. The first morning of the holidays, it had been really weird getting up and having breakfast with Olly's family, but nobody had batted an eyelid, and Scott's vague embarrassment hadn't lasted long.

Tonight, though, he'd be back in his own house. It was Christmas Eve and his older brother, Jamie, was coming home today with his fiancée. Scott wanted to spend Christmas Day with his family, although he and Olly were planning on seeing each other in the evening.

He shifted a little, finally opening his eyes and blinking. The light in the room was weird, brighter than usual. Maybe they'd slept in.

With a soft grunt, Olly stirred and lifted his head to look blearily at Scott. "Hey." His voice was rough with sleep.

"Morning."

They grinned lazily at each other.

"I love you," Olly said and shuffled up so he could reach Scott's lips for a kiss.

"Love you too," Scott said when they broke apart.

This was another thing he never got tired of. Since they'd started saying those words out loud, Scott loved hearing them.

"Come here." Olly rolled onto his side and took Scott with him for another kiss, more insistent this time as he pressed his thigh between Scott's, starting a slow grind against his hip. He reached a hand down to cup the bulge in Scott's underwear, pressing the heel of his hand against Scott's rapidly filling dick.

Scott liked where this was going. Lazy morning hand jobs with snogging were one of his favourite things.

But then an excited shriek from the landing outside distracted them.

"Oh my God! There's snow!" Sophie's voice. She hammered on Olly's door. "Get up, come and see. There's loads of it, and it wasn't forecast at all. This is *awesome*."

Snow where they lived was so unusual, it was even exciting enough to trump orgasms—just. "Seriously?" Olly called. "You'd better not be kidding."

"No, look." Sophie burst into the room and Scott was very glad they were still covered by the duvet. She went to the blind and opened it. Sudden white light flooded in. It pierced Scott's eyes and made him wince and blink until they adjusted.

"Fuck." Olly sat up, squinting out the window. "She's right. That's a *lot* of snow."

"I'm going out in it right now," Sophie said decisively, "before it gets all trodden on and spoilt. Are you coming?"

Olly looked down at Scott and raised his eyebrows. "You up for a snowball fight before breakfast?"

"Hell yes." Scott grinned.

The snowball fight was a savage free-for-all. Scott used his weight advantage to pin Olly several times and shove snow down his back. But Olly threw with dangerous accuracy, and Sophie proved that blood was thicker than water by ganging up with Olly to take Scott down. They got him face down in the snow, and Olly sat on him while Sophie shoved handfuls of snow up Scott's T-shirt until he was yelling for mercy.

"You bastards." He rolled onto his back when Olly finally got off him. "Two against one is so not fair."

"You're bigger than us. It's totally fair." Olly offered a hand to pull him up. So of course, Scott pulled Olly back down and rolled him over and over in the snow until they were both breathless and laughing.

"You've got snow in your hair." Scott grinned up at Olly.

"I've got snow everywhere." Olly kissed him, and his lips were cold, but his tongue was warm.

A snowball exploding against the side of Olly's head showered Scott with yet more flakes.

"Oi!" Olly broke the kiss to glare at a grinning Sophie.

When cold and hunger won out over the novelty of the snow, they went back inside for a while. A change of clothes, bacon sandwiches, and hot cups of tea helped them thaw out.

"Shall we go and see if Miss Wychwood's in?" Olly asked once they'd cleared their dirty plates away.

"Yes. Let's."

They'd been home for a few days now but hadn't visited Miss Wychwood yet. Over the summer they'd got to know her better once they got over their nervousness around her. As promised, they'd gone back to see her after their exams, and that time they accepted her offer of lemonade.

When they noticed her struggling with her lawnmower one day, Olly offered to cut the grass on her front lawn for her, and she accepted gratefully. Meanwhile, Scott cut back some of the larger shrubs in her garden, and after that they regularly popped round to help her in the garden. She always rewarded them with her lemonade and homemade biscuits or cake afterwards, and they developed a tentative friendship with her.

Her cat, Rowan, was always pleased to see them. Scott was a little smug about the fact that he seemed to be Rowan's favourite—his was usually the first choice of lap.

It had started to snow again when they walked around to Miss Wychwood's front door. Feathery flakes drifted from a slate grey sky, settling over the footprints on the pavement and the tyre tracks in the street.

Rowan was sitting on the doorstep when they arrived, as though he was waiting for them. He wrapped himself around Scott's ankles with an imperious "Miaow."

"Hello," Scott said.

As Olly rang the bell, Scott tucked the plant they'd brought as a gift carefully in one arm and stooped to scratch Rowan on his sleek black head.

They'd bought a beautiful amaryllis with scarlet blooms that were on the cusp of opening. Another plant had seemed like a safe bet, given Miss Wychwood's love of all growing things.

The front door creaked open and she greeted them with a delighted smile. "Boys! How lovely. Come in, come in." She ushered them inside, and Rowan came too, still rubbing himself against Scott's legs.

"Merry Christmas." Olly offered her the plant. It had a big gold ribbon tied around the pot and looked very festive.

"We got something for Rowan too." Scott grinned, feeling a little daft at buying a present for a cat. But there had been a pet gift display in the garden centre where they'd bought the plant, and Scott couldn't resist the catnip mice with bells inside them. He held Rowan's mouse up by its tail. "Sorry it's not wrapped."

She chuckled. "I don't think Rowan will mind. Come through to the back room, and you can give it to him there."

She led them through the dark hallway and out to the room at the back of the house. It hadn't changed in the seven years since Scott had first seen it. The walls were the same shade of green and plants lined the windowsill and mantelpiece. The crystal sphere drew his gaze, still in pride of place in the centre. A fire crackled in the grate and the room was lovely and warm.

Miss Wychwood put the new plant down on a bookshelf, next to the one they'd given her in the summer. "Have a seat. What would you like to drink? It's a little cold for lemonade today, I think. Would you like tea, or cocoa? And I have some mince pies too."

"Cocoa sounds great, thanks," Olly replied.

"Same for me, please." Scott sat beside Olly on the shabby old sofa, and Miss Wychwood pottered off to the kitchen. "Here, Rowan." He jingled the bell at the cat.

Rowan's ears pricked up and he came to investigate. He sniffed the catnip mouse, and Scott wiggled it, dangling it by its tail. With a swipe of his claws, Rowan snatched it from Scott's hand. He held it between his two front paws, rubbed his face on it, and then batted it across the floor and pounced.

"That should keep him busy for a while." Olly chuckled.

Scott turned to Olly and his breath caught. Intent on Rowan, Olly didn't notice Scott's scrutiny at first. As Olly smiled in amusement at the cat's antics, his face was alight, his dark hair falling into his eyes. Scott reached to brush it away, still amazed that Olly was his to touch now.

Olly caught his hand and held it, his attention all on Scott. "Remember the time we lost our football and climbed over to get it?"

Scott nodded. "I was so scared when she caught us."

"That was when all this began, I think." Olly had a faraway look in his eyes. "Maybe if you hadn't booted the ball over the fence that day, none of this would ever have happened."

Scott ran his thumb over the scar on Olly's wrist that matched the one on his own.

Best friends forever.

"In that case. I'm really glad I kicked it over."

"Me too." Olly leaned in and kissed Scott lightly on the lips. "If we could go back in time, I wouldn't change a thing."

About the Author

Jay lives just outside Bristol in the West of England, with her husband, two children, and two cats. Jay comes from a family of writers, but she always used to believe that the gene for fiction writing had passed her by. She spent years only ever writing emails, articles, or website content.

One day, she decided to try and write a short story—just to see if she could—and found it rather addictive. She hasn't stopped writing since.

Connect with Jay

www.jaynorthcote.com
Twitter: @Jay_Northcote
Facebook: Jay Northcote Fiction

More from Jay Northcote

Novels and Novellas
Cold Feet
Nothing Serious
Nothing Special
Nothing Ventured
Not Just Friends
Passing Through
The Little Things
The Dating Game – Owen & Nathan #1
The Marrying Kind – Owen & Nathan #2
Helping Hand – Housemates #1
Like a Lover – Housemates #2
Practice Makes Perfect – Housemates #3
What Happens at Christmas
The Law of Attraction
Imperfect Harmony

Short Stories (ebook only)
Top Me Maybe?
All Man

Free Reads (ebook only)
Coming Home
First Class Package
Why Love Matters

Jay also has several titles available in audiobook via Audible, Amazon or Apple.

Made in the USA
Charleston, SC
21 November 2016